GREAT ILLUSTRATED CLASSICS

CINDERELLA
& Other Stories

ABDO
Publishing Company

GREAT ILLUSTRATED CLASSICS

edited by
Rochelle Larkin

visit us at
www.abdopub.com

Library edition published in 2005 by ABDO Publishing Company, 4940 Viking Drive, Suite 622, Edina, Minnesota 55435. Published by agreement with Playmore Incorporated Publishers and Waldman Publishing Corporation.

Library of Congress Cataloging-in-Publication Data

Cinderella & other stories / [edited by Rochelle Larkin].
    p. cm. -- (Great illustrated classics)
  "First classics edition"--Cover.
  Contents: Cinderella -- Jack the giant killer -- Tom Thumb -- The ugly duckling - The dragon and his grandmother -- Rumpelstiltskin -- Pinkel the thief - The enchanted wreath -- Princess Mayblossom -- How Moti won the war.
  ISBN 1-59679-239-6
  1. Fairy Tales. [1. Fairy tales. 2. Folklore.] I. Title: Cinderella and other stories. II. Larkin, Rochelle. III. Series.

PZ8.C4888 2005
[398.2]--dc22

2004062304

Contents

She Could Not Bear This Pretty Girl.

CINDERELLA

O nce there was a gentleman who married, for his second wife, the proudest and most haughty woman that was ever seen. She had, by a former husband, two daughters who were, indeed, exactly like her in all things. He had likewise, by his first wife, a young daughter, but of unparalleled goodness and sweetness of temper, which she took from her mother, who had been the best creature in the world.

No sooner were the wedding ceremonies over but the new mother began to show herself in her true colors. She could not bear the good qualities of this pretty girl, and the less because they made her own daughters appear the worst.

She employed her in the work of the house: the girl scoured the dishes, tables, and madam's chamber, and those of her daughters; she slept in a sorry garret, upon a wretched straw bed, while her sisters lay in fine rooms, with floors all inlaid, upon beds of the very newest fashion, and where they had looking-glasses so large that they might see themselves from head to foot.

CINDERELLA

The poor girl bore all patiently, and dared not tell her father, for his wife governed him entirely. When she had done her work, she used to go into the chimney-corner, and sit down among cinders and ashes, which made her be called Cinderella. However, Cinderella, notwithstanding her mean apparel, was a hundred times prettier than her sisters, though they were always dressed very richly.

It happened that the King's son gave a ball, and invited all persons of fashion to it. Our young misses were also invited, for they cut a very grand figure. They were mightily delighted at this invitation, and wonderfully busy in choosing out such gowns, petticoats, and headdresses as might become them. This was a new trouble for Cinderella; for it was she who ironed her sisters' linen, and smoothed their ruffles; they talked all day long of nothing but how they should be dressed.

"For my part," said the eldest, "I will wear my red velvet suit with French trimming."

"And I," said the youngest, "shall have my usual petticoat; but then, to make amends for that, I will put on my gold-flowered mantle, and my diamond belt, which is far from being the most ordinary one in the world."

They sent for the best woman they could get to make up their headdresses and adjust their skirts, and make them look as good as they possibly could.

Cinderella was likewise called up to them to be consulted in

A New Trouble for Cinderella

all these matters, for she had excellent notions, and advised them always for the best, and offered her services to dress their hair, which they were very willing she should do. As she was doing this, they said to her:

"Cinderella, would you not be glad to go to the ball?"

"Alas!" said she. "You only jeer at me; it is not for such as I am to go."

"You are right," replied they; "it would make the people laugh to see a cindergirl at a ball."

Anyone but Cinderella would have dressed their heads awry, but she was very good, and dressed them perfectly well. They were almost two days without eating, so much they were transported with joy. They broke above a dozen laces in trying to be laced up close, that they might have fine slender shapes, and they were continually at their looking-glass. At last the happy day came; they went to court, and Cinderella followed them with her eyes as long as she could, and when she had lost sight of them, she fell a-crying.

Her godmother, who saw her all in tears, asked her what was the matter.

"I wish I could — I wish I could — " she was not able to speak the rest, being interrupted by her tears and sobbing.

This godmother of hers, who was a fairy, said to her, "Thou wishest thou couldst go to the ball, is it not so?"

"Y—es," cried Cinderella, with a great sigh.

"Well," said her godmother, "be a good girl, and I will make

Her Godmother Asked What Was the Matter.

it that thou shalt go." Then she took her into her chamber, and said to her, "Run into the garden, and bring me a pumpkin."

Cinderella went immediately to gather the finest she could get, and brought it to her godmother, not being able to imagine how this pumpkin could help her go to the ball. Her godmother scooped out all the inside of it, having left nothing but the rind; which done, she struck it with her wand, and the pumpkin was instantly turned into a fine coach, gilded all over with gold.

She then went to look into her mouse-trap, where she found six mice, all alive, and ordered Cinderella to lift up a little the trap-door; then, giving each mouse, as it went out, a little tap with her wand, the mouse was that moment turned into a fine horse, which altogether made a very fine set of six horses of a beautiful mouse-colored dapple-grey.

"Being at a loss for a coachman, I will go and see," Cinderella said, "if there is a rat in the rat-trap — we may make a coachman of him."

"Thou art in the right," replied her godmother; "go and look." Cinderella brought the trap to her, and in it there were three huge rats. The fairy picked the one which had the largest beard, and, having touched him with her wand, he was turned into a fat, jolly coachman, who had the smartest whiskers eyes ever beheld.

After that, she said to her: "Go again into the garden, and you will find six lizards behind the watering-pot. Bring them to me."

Cinderella had no sooner done so but her godmother turned

"Bring Me a Pumpkin."

them into six footmen, who skipped up immediately behind the coach, with their liveries all gold and silver, and clung as close behind each other as if they had done nothing else their whole lives. The fairy then said to Cinderella:

"Well, you see here an equipage fit to go to the ball with; are you not pleased with it?"

"Oh! Yes," cried Cinderella; "but must I go thither as I am, in these nasty rags?"

Her godmother only just touched her with her wand, and, at the same instant, her clothes were turned into cloth of gold and silver, all set with jewels. This done, she gave her a pair of glass slippers, the prettiest in the whole world.

Being thus dressed, she got up into her coach; but her godmother commanded her not to stay after midnight, above all things telling her, at the same time, that if she stayed one moment longer, the coach would be a pumpkin again, her horses mice, her coachman a rat, her footmen lizards, and her clothes become just as they were before.

She promised her godmother she would not fail to leave the ball before midnight; and then away she drove, scarce able to contain herself for joy.

The King's son, who was told that a great Princess, whom nobody knew, was come, ran out to receive her; he gave her his hand as she alighted out of the coach, and led her into the hall, among all the company.

A Pair of Glass Slippers

There was immediately a profound silence. They left off dancing, and the violins ceased to play, so attentive was everyone to contemplate the singular beauties of the unknown newcomer.

Nothing was then heard but a murmured noise of: "How handsome she is! How handsome she is!"

The King himself, old as he was, could not help watching her, and telling the Queen softly that it was a long time since he had seen so beautiful and lovely a creature.

All the ladies were busied in considering her clothes and headdress, that they might have some made next day after the same pattern, provided they could meet with such fine materials and as able hands to make them.

The King's son conducted her to the most honorable seat, and afterwards took her out to dance with him; she danced so very gracefully that they all more and more admired her. A fine dinner was served up, whereof the young Prince ate not a morsel, so intently was he busied in gazing on her.

She went and sat down by her sisters, showing them a thousand civilities, giving them part of the oranges and citrons which the Prince had presented her with, which very much surprised them, for they did not know her. While Cinderella was thus amusing her sisters, she heard the clock strike eleven and three-quarters, whereupon she immediately made a curtsey to the company and hastened away as fast as she could.

Being home, she ran to seek out her godmother, and, after

The King's Son Took Her Out to Dance.

having thanked her, she said she could not but wish she might go next day to the second ball, as the King's son had desired her to.

As she was eagerly telling her godmother whatever had passed at the ball, her two sisters knocked at the door, which Cinderella ran and opened.

"How long you have stayed!" cried she, gaping and rubbing her eyes and stretching herself as if she had been just waked out of her sleep.

"If thou hadst been at the ball," said one of her sisters, "thou wouldst not have been tired of it. There came thither the finest Princess, the most beautiful ever seen with mortal eyes; she showed us a thousand civilities, and gave us oranges and citrons."

Cinderella seemed very indifferent in the matter; indeed, she asked them the name of that Princess; but they told her they did not know it, and that the King's son was very uneasy on that account and would give all the world to know who she was.

At this Cinderella, smiling, replied: "She must, then, be very beautiful indeed; how happy you have been! Could not I see her? Ah! Dear Miss Charlotte, do lend me your yellow suit of clothes which you wear every day."

"Ay, to be sure!" cried Miss Charlotte. "Lend my clothes to such a dirty cindergirl as thou art! I should be a fool."

Cinderella, indeed, well expected such an answer, and was very glad of the refusal; for she would have been sadly put to it if her sister had lent her what she asked for in jest!

"How Long You Have Stayed!"

CINDERELLA

The next day the two sisters were at the ball, and so was Cinderella, but dressed more magnificently than before. The King's son was always by her, and never ceased his compliments and kind speeches to her; for Cinderella this was so far from being tiresome that she quite forgot what her godmother had told her; so that she counted the clock striking twelve when she took it to be no more than eleven; she then rose up and fled, as nimble as a deer.

The Prince followed, but could not overtake her. She left behind one of her glass slippers, which the Prince took up most carefully.

She got home, but quite out of breath, and in her nasty old clothes, having nothing left her of all her finery but one of the little slippers, the mate to that she dropped.

The guards at the palace gate were asked if they had not seen a Princess go out. But they said they had seen nobody go out but a young girl, very meanly dressed, and who had more the air of a poor country wench than a gentlewoman.

When the two sisters returned from the ball, Cinderella asked them if they had been well entertained, and if the fine lady had been there.

They told her yes, but that she hurried away immediately at midnight, and with so much haste that she dropped one of her little glass slippers, which the King's son had taken up; that he had done nothing but look at her all the time at the ball, and that most

One of Her Glass Slippers

certainly he was very much in love with the beautiful person who owned the glass slipper.

What they said was very true; a few days after, the King's son caused it to be proclaimed, by sound of trumpet, that he would marry her whose foot this slipper would fit. They whom he employed began to try it upon the Princesses, then the Duchesses and all the court, but in vain; it was brought to the two sisters, who did all they possibly could to thrust a foot into the slipper, but they could not do it.

Cinderella, who saw all this, and knew her slipper, said to them, laughing: "Let me see if it will not fit me."

Her sisters burst out a-laughing, and began to banter her. The gentleman who was sent to try the slipper looked earnestly at Cinderella, and, finding her very handsome, said it was but just that she should try, and that he had orders to let everyone make trial.

He obliged Cinderella to sit down, and, putting the slipper to her foot, he found it went on very easily, and fitted her as if it had been made for her. The astonishment her two sisters were in was excessively great, but still abundantly greater when Cinderella pulled out of her pocket the other slipper, and put it on her foot.

Thereupon, in came her godmother, who, having touched with her wand Cinderella's clothes, made them richer and more magnificent than any of those she had before.

And now her two sisters found her to be that fine, beautiful lady whom they had seen at the ball. They threw themselves at her

Putting the Slipper to Her Foot

feet to beg pardon for all the ill treatment they had made her undergo.

Cinderella took them up, and, as she embraced them, cried that she forgave them with all her heart, and desired them always to love her.

She was conducted to the young Prince, dressed as she was; he thought her more charming than ever, and, a few days after, married her. Cinderella, who was no less good than beautiful, gave her two sisters lodgings in the palace, and that very same day married them to two great lords of the court.

No Less Good Than Beautiful

Cormoran!

JACK · THE · GIANT-KILLER

When good King Arthur reigned, there lived near the Land's End of England, in the county of Cornwall, a farmer who had only one son called Jack. He was brisk and of a ready lively wit, so that nobody or nothing could best him.

In those days the Mount of Cornwall was kept by a huge giant named Cormoran. He was eighteen feet in height, and about three yards round the waist, of a fierce and grim countenance, the terror of all the neighboring towns and villages. He lived in a cave in the midst of the Mount, and whenever he wanted food he would wade over to the mainland, where he would furnish himself with whatever came in his way. Everybody at his approach ran out of their houses, while he seized their cattle, making nothing of carrying half-a-dozen oxen on his back at a time; and as for their sheep and hogs, he would tie them round his waist like a bunch of tallow-dips. He had done this for many years, so that all Cornwall was in despair.

JACK THE GIANT-KILLER

One day Jack happened to be at the town-hall when the magistrates were sitting in council about the giant. He asked: "What reward will be given to the man who kills Cormoran?"

"The giant's treasure," they said, "will be the reward."

Quoth Jack: "Then let me undertake it."

So he got a horn, shovel, and pickax, and went over to the Mount in the beginning of a dark winter's evening, when he fell to work, and before morning had dug a pit twenty-two feet deep, and nearly as broad, covering it over with long sticks and straw. Then he strewed a little mold over it, so that it appeared like plain ground.

Jack then placed himself on the opposite side of the pit, farthest from the giant's lodging, and, just at the break of day, he put the horn to his mouth, and blew, *Tantivy, Tantivy.*

This noise roused the giant, who rushed from his cave, crying: "You incorrigible villain, are you come here to disturb my rest? You shall pay dearly for this. Satisfaction I will have, and this it shall be, I will take you whole and broil you for breakfast."

He had no sooner uttered this, than he tumbled into the pit, and made the very foundations of the Mount shake.

"Oh, Giant," quoth Jack, "where are you now? Oh, faith, you are now in Lob's Pound, where I will plague you for your threatening words: what do you think now of broiling me for your breakfast? Will no other diet serve you but poor Jack?" Then having teased the giant for a while, he gave him a most weighty knock

Rousing the Giant

with his pickax on the very crown of his head, and killed him on the spot.

Jack then filled up the pit with earth, and went to search the cave, which he found contained much treasure. When the magistrates heard of this they made a declaration he should henceforth be termed

JACK THE GIANT-KILLER

and presented him with a sword and a belt, on which were written these words embroidered in letters of gold:

> "Here's the right valiant Cornish man,
>
> Who slew the giant Cormoran."

The news of Jack's victory soon spread over all the West of England, so that another giant, named Blunderbore, hearing of it, vowed to be revenged on Jack, if ever he should meet him. This giant was the lord of an enchanted castle situated in the midst of a lonesome wood.

Now Jack, about four months afterwards, walking near this wood in his journey to Wales, being weary, seated himself near a pleasant fountain and fell fast asleep. While he was sleeping, the giant, coming there for water, discovered him, and knew him to be the far-famed Jack the Giant-killer by the lines written on the belt.

He took Jack on his shoulders and carried him towards his castle. Now, as they passed through a thicket, the rustling of the boughs awakened Jack, who was strangely surprised to find him-

He Took Jack on His Shoulders.

self in the clutches of the giant. His terror had only begun, for, on entering the castle, he saw the ground strewed with human bones, and the giant told him his own would before long be among them.

After this the giant locked poor Jack in an immense chamber, leaving him there while he went to fetch another giant, his brother, living in the same wood, who might share in the meal of Jack.

After waiting some time, Jack, on going to the window, beheld afar off the two giants coming towards the castle. "Now," quoth Jack to himself, "my death or my deliverance is at hand."

Now there were strong cords in a corner of the room in which Jack was, and two of these he took, and made a strong noose at the ends; and while the giants were unlocking the iron gate of the castle he threw the ropes over each of their heads. Then he drew the other ends across a beam, and pulled with all his might, so that he throttled them. When he saw they were black in the face, he slid down the rope, and drawing his sword, slew them both. Then, taking the giant's keys, and unlocking the rooms, he found three fair ladies tied by the hair of their heads, almost starved to death. "Sweet ladies," quoth Jack, "I have destroyed this monster and his brutish brother, and obtained your liberties." This said, he presented them with the keys, and so proceeded on his journey to Wales.

Jack made the best of his way by travelling as fast as he could, but lost his way, and was confused, and could find no habitation until, coming into a narrow valley, he found a large house, and in

Fetching His Brother Giant

order to get shelter took courage to knock at the gate.

But what was his surprise when there came forth a monstrous giant with two heads; yet he did nòt appear so fiery as the others were, for he was a Welsh giant, and what bad he did was by secret malice under the false show of friendship.

Jack, having told his condition to the giant, was shown into a bedroom, where, in the dead of night, he heard his host in another apartment muttering these words:

"Though here you lodge with me this night,
You shall not see the morning light:
My club shall find your head outright!"

"Say'st thou so," quoth Jack; "that is one of your tricks, yet I hope to be cunning enough for you." Then, getting out of bed, he laid a bundle in the bed in his stead, and hid himself in a corner of the room. At the dead time of the night in came the giant, who struck several heavy blows on the bed with his club, thinking he had broken every bone in Jack's skin.

The next morning Jack, laughing in his sleeve, gave him hearty thanks for his night's lodging.

"How have you rested?" quoth the giant. "Did you not feel anything in the night?"

"No," quoth Jack, "nothing but a rat, which gave me two or three slaps with her tail."

With that, greatly wondering, the giant led Jack to breakfast, bringing him a bowl containing four gallons of thick pudding.

Monstrous!

JACK THE GIANT-KILLER

Not wanting to let the giant think it too much for him, Jack put a large leather bag under his loose coat, in such a way that he could convey the pudding into it without its being perceived.

Then, telling the giant he would show him a trick, taking a knife, Jack ripped open the bag, and out came all the pudding. Whereupon, saying, "Odds splutters, I can do that trick myself," the monster took the knife, and ripping open his own belly, fell down dead.

Now, it happened in these days that King Arthur's only son asked his father to give him a large sum of money, in order that he might go and seek his fortune in the principality of Wales, where lived a beautiful lady possessed with seven evil spirits. The King did his best to persuade his son from it, but in vain; so at last gave way and the Prince set out with two horses, one loaded with money, the other for himself to ride upon.

Now, after several days' travel, he came to a market-town in Wales, where he beheld a vast crowd of people gathered together.

The Prince asked the reason of it, and was told that they had arrested a corpse for several large sums of money which he owed when he died. The prince replied that it was a pity creditors should be so cruel, and said: "Go bury the dead, and let his creditors come to my lodging, and their debts shall be paid." They came in such great numbers that before night he had only twopence left for himself.

Now Jack the Giant-killer, coming that way, was so taken

Jack Ripped Open the Bag.

with the generosity of the Prince, that he desired to be his servant. This being agreed upon, the next morning they set forward on their journey together, when, as they were riding out of the town, an old woman called after the Prince, saying, "He has owed me twopence these seven years; pray pay me as well as the rest." Putting his hand to his pocket, the Prince gave the woman all he had left, so that after their day's food, which cost what small store Jack had by him, they were without a penny between them.

When the sun got low, the King's son said: "Jack, since we have no money, where can we lodge this night?"

But Jack replied: "Master, we'll do well enough, for I have an uncle who lives within two miles of this place; he is a huge and monstrous giant with three heads; he'll fight five hundred men in armor, and make them fly before him."

"Alas!" quoth the Prince, "what shall we do there? He'll certainly chop us up at a mouthful. Nay, we are scarce enough to fill one of his hollow teeth!"

"It is no matter for that," quoth Jack; "I myself will go before and prepare the way for you; therefore stop here and wait till I return."

Jack then rode away at full speed, and coming to the gate of the castle, he knocked so loud that he made the neighboring hills resound.

The giant roared out at this like thunder: "Who's there?"

Jack answered: "None but your poor cousin Jack."

"Where Can We Lodge This Night?"

Quoth he: "What news has my poor cousin Jack?"

Jack replied: "Dear uncle, heavy news, I fear!"

"Prithee," quoth the giant, "what heavy news can come to me? I am a giant with three heads, and besides thou knowest I can fight five hundred men in armor, and make them fly like chaff before the wind."

"Oh, but," quoth Jack, "here's the King's son a-coming with a thousand men in armor to kill you and destroy all that you have!"

"Oh, cousin Jack," said the giant, "this is heavy news indeed! I will immediately run and hide myself, and thou shalt lock, bolt, and bar me in, and keep the keys until the Prince is gone."

Having secured the giant, Jack fetched his master, and they made themselves heartily merry whilst the poor giant lay trembling in a vault under the ground.

Early in the morning Jack furnished his master with a fresh supply of gold and silver, and then sent him three miles forward on his journey, at which time the Prince was pretty well out of the smell of the giant.

Jack then returned, and let the giant out of the vault, who asked what he should give Jack for keeping the castle from destruction.

"Why," quoth Jack, "I want nothing but the old coat and cap, together with the old rusty sword and slippers which are at your bed's head."

Quoth the giant: "You know not what you ask; they are the

What Heavy News Can Come to Me?

most precious things I have. The coat will keep you invisible, the cap will tell you all you want to know, the sword cuts asunder whatever you strike, and the shoes are of extraordinary swiftness. But you have been very serviceable to me, therefore take them with all my heart."

Jack thanked his uncle, and then went off with them. He soon overtook his master and they quickly arrived at the house of the lady the Prince sought, who, finding the Prince to be a suitor, prepared a splendid banquet for him.

After the repast was concluded, she told him she had a task for him. She wiped his mouth with a handkerchief, saying, "You must show me that handkerchief to-morrow morning, or else you will lose your head." With that she put it in her pocket.

The Prince went to bed in great sorrow, but Jack's cap of knowledge informed him how it was to be obtained. In the middle of the night she called upon a spirit to carry her to a demon. But Jack put on his coat of darkness and his shoes of swiftness, and was there as soon as she was.

When she entered the place of the demon, she gave the handkerchief to him, and he laid it upon a shelf, whence Jack took it and brought it to his master, who showed it to the lady next day, and so saved his life.

On that, she gave the Prince a kiss and told him he must show her the lips tomorrow morning that she would kiss that night, or lose his head.

The Coat of Darkness, the Shoes of Swiftness

"Ah!" he replied, "if you kiss none but mine, I will."

"That is neither here nor there," said she; "if you do not, death's your portion!"

At midnight she went as before, and was angry with the demon for letting the handkerchief go. "But now," quoth she, "I will be too hard for the King's son, for I will kiss thee, and he is to show me thy lips." Which she did, and Jack, when she was not standing by, cut off the demon's head and brought it under his invisible coat to his master, who the next morning pulled it out by the horns before the lady.

This broke the enchantment and the evil spirit left her, and she appeared in all her beauty. They were married the next morning, and soon after went to the court of King Arthur, where Jack, for his many great exploits, was made one of the Knights of the Round Table.

Jack soon went searching for giants again, but he had not ridden far when he saw a cave, near the entrance of which he beheld a giant sitting upon a block of timber, with a knotted iron club by his side. His eyes were like flames of fire, his countenance grim and ugly, and his cheeks like a couple of large flitches of bacon, while the bristles of his beard resembled rods of iron wire, and the locks that hung down upon his brawny shoulders were like curled snakes or hissing adders.

Jack alighted from his horse, and, putting on the coat of darkness, went up close to the giant, and said softly: "Oh! are you

The Enchantment Broken

there? It will not be long before I take you fast by the beard."

The giant all this while could not see him, on account of his invisible coat, so that Jack, coming up close to the monster, struck a blow with his sword at his head, but, missing his aim, he cut off the nose instead. At this, the giant roared like claps of thunder, and began to lay about him with his iron club like one stark mad.

But Jack, running behind, drove his sword up to the hilt in the giant's back, so that he fell down dead. This done, Jack cut off the giant's head, and sent it to King Arthur, by a wagoner he hired for that purpose.

Jack now resolved to enter the giant's cave in search of his treasure, and, passing along through a great many windings and turnings, he came at length to a large room paved with freestone, at the upper end of which was a boiling caldron, and on the right hand a large table, at which the giant used to dine. Then he came to a window, barred with iron, through which he looked and beheld a vast number of miserable captives, who, seeing him, cried out: "Alas! young man, art thou come to be one amongst us in this miserable den?"

"Ay," quoth Jack, "but pray tell me what is the meaning of your captivity?"

"We are kept here," said one, "till such time as the giants have a wish to feast, and then the fattest among us is slaughtered! And many are the times they have dined upon men!"

"Say you so," quoth Jack, and straightway unlocked the gate

In Search of Treasure

and let them free, who all rejoiced like condemned men at sight of a pardon. Then searching the giant's coffers, he shared the gold and silver equally amongst them and took them to a neighboring castle, where they all feasted and made merry over their deliverance.

But in the midst of all this mirth a messenger brought news that one Thunderdell, a giant with two heads, having heard of the death of his kinsmen, had come from the north to be revenged on Jack, and was within a mile of the castle, the country people flying before him like chaff.

But Jack was not a bit daunted, and said: "Let him come! I have a tool to pick his teeth; and you, ladies and gentlemen, walk out into the garden, and you shall witness this giant Thunderdell's death and destruction."

The castle was situated in the midst of a small island surrounded by a moat thirty feet deep and twenty feet wide, over which lay a drawbridge. So Jack employed men to cut through this bridge on both sides, nearly to the middle; and then, dressing himself in his invisible coat, he marched against the giant with his sword of sharpness.

Although the giant could not see Jack, he smelled his approach, and cried out in these words:

"Fee, fi, fo, fum!
I smell the blood of an Englishman!
Be he alive or be he dead,
I'll grind his bones to make my bread!"

"I Smell the Blood of an Englishman!"

"Say'st thou so," said Jack; "then thou art a monstrous miller indeed."

The giant cried out again: "Art thou that villain who killed my kinsmen? Then I will tear thee with my teeth, and grind thy bones to powder."

"You'll have to catch me first," quoth Jack, and throwing off his invisible coat, so that the giant might see him, and putting on his shoes of swiftness, he ran from the giant, who followed like a walking castle, so that the very foundations of the earth seemed to shake at every step.

Jack led him a long dance, in order that the gentlemen and ladies might see; and at last to end the matter, ran lightly over the drawbridge, the giant, in full speed, pursuing him with his club. Then, coming to the middle of the bridge, the giant's great weight broke it down, and he tumbled headlong into the water, where he rolled and wallowed like a whale.

Jack, standing by the moat, laughed at him all the while; but though the giant foamed to hear him scoff, and plunged from place to place in the moat, yet he could not get out to be revenged. Jack at length got a cart-rope and cast it over the two heads of the giant, and drew him ashore by a team of horses, and then cut off both his heads with his sword of sharpness, and sent them to King Arthur.

After some time spent in mirth and pastime, Jack, taking leave of the knights and ladies, set out for new adventures. Through many woods he passed, and came at length to the foot of a high

"You'll Have to Catch Me First!"

mountain. Here, late at night, he found a lonesome house, and knocked at the door, which was opened by an aged man with a head as white as snow.

"Father," said Jack, "can you lodge a benighted traveller that has lost his way?"

"Yes," said the old man; "you are right welcome to my poor cottage."

Whereupon Jack entered, and down they sat together, and the old man began to speak as follows:

"Son, I see by your belt you are the great conqueror of giants, and behold, my son, on the top of this mountain is an enchanted castle, kept by a giant named Galligantua, and he by the help of an old conjurer, betrays many knights and ladies into his castle, where by magic art they are transformed into sundry shapes and forms.

"But above all, I grieve for a duke's daughter, whom they fetched from her father's garden, carrying her through the air in a burning chariot drawn by fiery dragons, and when they secured her within the castle, they transformed her into a white hare. And though many knights have tried to break the enchantment, and work her deliverance, yet no one could accomplish it, on account of two dreadful griffins which are placed at the castle gate and which destroy every one who comes near. But you, my son, may pass by them undiscovered, where on the gates of the castle you will find engraven in large letters how the spell may be broken."

An Enchanted Castle

Jack gave the old man his hand, and promised that in the morning he would venture his life to free the lady.

In the morning Jack arose and put on his invisible coat and magic cap and shoes, and prepared himself for the fray. Now, when he had reached the top of the mountain he soon discovered the two fiery griffins, but passed them without fear, because of his invisible coat. When he had got beyond them, he found upon the gates of the castle a golden trumpet hung by a silver chain, under which these lines were engraved:

> "Whoever shall this trumpet blow,
> Shall soon the giant overthrow,
> And break the bad enchantment straight;
> So all shall be in happy state."

Jack had no sooner read this but he blew the trumpet, at which the castle trembled to its vast foundations, and the giant and conjurer were in horrid confusion, biting their thumbs and tearing their hair, knowing their wicked reign was at an end.

Then the giant stooping to take up his club, Jack at one blow cut off his head; whereupon the conjurer, mounting up into the air, was carried away in a whirlwind. Then the enchantment was broken, and all the lords and ladies who had so long been transformed into birds and beasts returned to their proper shapes, and the castle vanished away in a cloud of smoke.

This being done, the head of Galligantua was likewise, in the usual manner, conveyed to the court of King Arthur, where, the

Two Fiery Griffins

very next day, Jack followed, with the knights and ladies who had been delivered. Whereupon, as a reward for his good services, the King prevailed upon the duke to bestow his daughter in marriage on honest Jack.

So married they were, and the whole kingdom was filled with joy at the wedding. Furthermore, the King bestowed on Jack a noble castle, with a very beautiful estate, where he and his lady lived in great joy and happiness all the rest of their days.

A Reward for Good Services

The Mighty Merlin

THE · HISTORY · OF · TOM · THUMB

*I*n the days of the great King Arthur, there lived a mighty magician, called Merlin, the most learned and skillful enchanter the world has ever seen.

This famous magician, who could take any form he pleased, was travelling about as a poor beggar, and being very tired, he stopped at the cottage of a ploughman to rest himself, and asked for some food.

The countryman bade him welcome, and his wife, who was a very good-hearted woman, soon brought him some milk in a wooden bowl, and some coarse brown bread on a platter.

Merlin was much pleased with the kindness of the ploughman and his wife; but he could not help noticing that though everything was neat and comfortable in the cottage, they both seemed to be very unhappy. He therefore asked them why they were so melancholy, and learned that they were miserable because they had no children.

The poor woman said, with tears in her eyes: "I should be the happiest creature in the world if I had a son; although he was no bigger than my thumb, I would be satisfied."

Merlin was so much amused with the idea of a boy no bigger than a thumb, that he determined to grant the poor woman's wish. Accordingly, in a short time after, the ploughman's wife had a son, who, wonderful to relate! was not a bit bigger than his mother's thumb.

The Queen of the fairies, wishing to see the little fellow, came in at the window while the mother was sitting up in the bed admiring him. The Queen kissed the child, and, giving him the name of Tom Thumb, sent for some of the fairies, who dressed her little godson according to her orders;

> "An oak-leaf hat he had for his crown;
> His shirt of web by spiders spun;
> With jacket wove of thistle's down;
> His trousers were of feathers done.
> His stockings, of apple-rind, they tie
> With eyelash from his mother's eye:
> His shoes were made of mouse's skin,
> Tann'd with the downy hair within."

Tom never grew any larger than a thumb of only ordinary size; but as he got older he became very cunning and full of tricks. When he was old enough to play with the boys, and had lost all his own cherry stones, he used to creep into the bags of his playfellows, fill his pockets, and, getting out without their noticing him,

A Boy no Bigger than a Thumb!

would again join in the game.

One day, however, as he was coming out of a bag of cherry-stones, where he had been stealing as usual, the boy to whom it belonged chanced to see him. "Ah, ah! my little Tommy," said the boy, "so I have caught you stealing my cherry-stones at last, and you shall be rewarded for your thievish tricks." On saying this, he drew the string tight round Tom's neck, and gave the bag such a hearty shake, that poor little Tom's legs, thighs, and body were sadly bruised. He roared out with pain, and begged to be let out, promising never to steal again.

A short time afterwards his mother was making a batter pudding, and Tom, being very anxious to see how it was made, climbed up to the edge of the bowl; but his foot slipped, and he plumped over head and ears into the batter, without his mother noticing him, who stirred him into the pudding, and put him in the pot to boil.

The batter filled Tom's mouth, and prevented him from crying; but, on feeling the hot water, he kicked and struggled so much in the pot that his mother thought that the pudding was bewitched, and, pulling it out of the pot, she threw it outside the door. A poor tinker, who was passing by, lifted up the pudding, and, putting it into his bag, he then walked off.

As Tom had now got his mouth cleared of the batter, he then began to cry aloud, which so frightened the tinker that he flung down the pudding and ran away. The pudding being broke to

Into the Batter!

pieces by the fall, Tom crept out covered all over with the batter, and walked home. His mother, who was very sorry to see her darling in such a woeful state, put him into a teacup, and soon washed off the batter; after which she kissed him, and laid him in bed.

Soon after the adventure of the pudding, Tom's mother went to milk her cow in the meadow, and she took him along with her. As the wind was very high, for fear of his being blown away she tied him to a thistle with a piece of fine thread. The cow soon observed Tom's oak-leaf hat, and liking the appearance of it, took poor Tom and the thistle at one mouthful. While the cow was chewing the thistle Tom was afraid of her great teeth, which threatened to crush him in pieces, and he roared out as loud as he could: "Mother, mother!"

"Where are you, Tommy, my dear Tommy?" asked his mother.

"Here, mother," replied he, "in the red cow's mouth."

His mother began to cry and wring her hands; but the cow, surprised at the odd noise in her throat, opened her mouth and let Tom drop out. Fortunately his mother caught him in her apron as he was falling to the ground, or he would have been dreadfully hurt. She then ran home with him.

Tom's father made him a whip out of a barley straw to drive the cattle with, and having one day gone into the fields, he slipped and rolled into the furrow. A raven, which was flying over, picked him up, and flew with him over the sea, and there dropped him.

A large fish swallowed Tom the moment he fell into the sea,

Liking the Look of It

which was soon after caught, and bought for the table of King Arthur. When they opened the fish in order to cook it, every one was astonished at finding such a little boy, and Tom was quite delighted at being free again.

They carried him to the King, who made Tom his dwarf, and he soon grew a great favorite at court; for by his tricks and gambols he not only amused the King and Queen, but also all the Knights of the Round Table.

It is said that when the King rode out on horseback, he often took Tom along with him, and if a shower came on, he used to creep into his majesty's waistcoat-pocket, where he slept till the rain was over.

King Arthur one day asked Tom about his parents, wishing to know if they were as small as he was, and whether they were well off. Tom told the King that his father and mother were as tall as anybody about the court, but in rather poor circumstances. On hearing this, the King carried Tom to his treasury, the place where he kept all his money, and told him to take as much money as he could carry home to his parents, which made the poor little fellow caper with joy. Tom went immediately to procure a purse, which was made of a water-bubble, and then returned to the treasury, where he received a silver threepenny piece to put into it.

Our little hero had some difficulty in lifting the burden upon his back; but he at last succeeded in getting it placed to his mind, and set forward on his journey. However, without meeting with

Astonished at Finding Tom

any accident, and after resting himself more than a hundred times by the way, in two days and two nights he reached his father's house in safety.

Tom had travelled forty-eight hours with a huge silver piece on his back, and was almost tired to death, when his mother ran out to meet him, and carried him into the house. But he soon returned to King Arthur's court.

As Tom's clothes had suffered much in the batter pudding, and the inside of the fish, his majesty ordered him a new suit of clothes, and to be mounted as a knight on a mouse.

> Of Butterfly's wings his shirt was made,
> His boots of chicken's hide;
> And by a nimble fairy blade,
> Well learned in the tailoring trade,
> His clothing was supplied.
> A needle dangled by his side;
> A dapper mouse he used to ride,
> Thus strutted Tom in stately pride!

It was certainly very diverting to see Tom in this dress and mounted on the mouse, as he rode out a-hunting with the King and nobility, who were all ready to expire with laughter at Tom and his fine prancing charger.

The King was so charmed with his appearance that he ordered a little chair to be made, in order that Tom might sit upon his table, and also a palace of gold, a span high, with a door an inch wide, to

Tom at Court

live in. He also gave him a coach, drawn by six small mice.

The Queen was so enraged at the honors conferred on Sir Thomas that she resolved to ruin him, and told the King that the little knight had been saucy to her.

The King sent for Tom in great haste, but being fully aware of the danger of royal anger, Tom crept into an empty snail-shell, where he lay for a long time until he was almost starved with hunger; but at last he ventured to peep out, and seeing a fine large butterfly on the ground, near the place of his concealment, he got close to it and jumping astride on it, was carried up into the air.

The butterfly flew with him from tree to tree and from field to field, and at last returned to the court, where the King and nobility all strove to catch him; but at last poor Tom fell from his seat into a watering-pot, in which he was almost drowned.

When the Queen saw him she was in a rage, and said he should be beheaded; and he was again put into a mouse trap until the time of his execution.

However a cat, observing something alive in the trap, patted it about till the wires broke, and set Thomas at liberty.

The King received Tom again into favor, which he did not live to enjoy, for a large spider one day attacked him; and although he drew his sword and fought well, the spider's poisonous breath at last overcame him.

He fell dead on the ground where he stood,
And the spider spilt every drop of his blood.

Jumping Astride

Here lies Tom Thumb
King Arthurs Knight

End

The End of Tom Thumb

THE HISTORY OF TOM THUMB

King Arthur and his whole court were so sorry at the loss of their little favorite that they went into mourning and raised a fine white marble monument over his grave with the following epitaph:

Here lies Tom Thumb, King Arthur's knight,
Who died by a spider's cruel bite.
He was well known in Arthur's court,
Where he afforded gallant sport;
He rode at tilt and tournament,
And on a mouse a-hunting went.
Alive he filled the court with mirth;
His death to sorrow soon gave birth.
Wipe, wipe your eyes, and shake your head
And cry, — Alas! Tom Thumb is dead!

Here Sat a Duck on Her Nest.

THE · UGLY · DUCKLING

by Hans Christian Andersen

I t was a glorious day in the country. It was summer, the corn-fields were yellow, the oats green, the hay had been put up in the green meadows, and the stork went about on his long red legs and chattered in Egyptian, the language he had learned from his mother. All around the fields and meadows were great forests, and in the midst of the forests were deep lakes.

In the midst of the sunshine lay an old farm, with deep canals, and from the wall down to the water grew great hedges, so high that little children could stand upright under the tallest of them. It was just as wild there as in the deepest wood.

Here sat a duck on her nest to hatch her ducklings. She was already tired even before the little ones came; and she seldom had visitors. The other ducks preferred to swim about rather than sit down under a hedge to gossip with her.

At last one eggshell after another burst open. "Peep! Peep!"

they cried, and soon in all the eggs there were little creatures that stuck out their heads.

"Quack! quack!" they said, and they all came quacking out as fast as they could, looking all round them at the green leaves. Their mother let them look as much as they chose, for green is good for the eye.

"How big the world is!" said all the ducklings, for they certainly had much more room now than when they were in the eggs.

"D'ye think this is all the world?" said the mother. "That stretch goes far across the other side of the garden, into the parson's field; I have never even been there yet. I hope you are all here," and she stood up. "No, not all. The largest egg still lies there. How long is that to last? I am really tired." And she sat down again.

"Well, how goes it?" asked an old duck who had come to pay her a visit.

"It's taking a long time with this one egg," said the mother duck. "It will not burst. Now, only look at the others. Are they not the prettiest little ducks one could possibly see? They are all like their father; the rogue never comes to see me."

"Let me see the egg which will not burst," said the old visitor. "You may be sure it is a turkey's egg. I was once cheated in that way, and had much trouble with the young ones, for they are afraid of the water. I could not get them to venture in. I quacked and I clacked, but it was no use. Let me see the egg. Yes, that's a turkey's egg. Let it lie there and go teach the other children to swim."

"The Largest Egg Still Lies There."

THE UGLY DUCKLING

"I think I will sit on it a little longer," said the duck. "I've sat so long now that I can sit a few days more."

"Just as you please," said the old duck; and away she went.

At last the great egg burst. "Peep! peep!" said the little one, and crept forth. It was very large and ugly. The duck looked at it.

"It's a very large duckling," said she, "none of the others look like that: can it really be a turkey chick? Well, we shall soon find out. It must go into the water, even if I have to thrust it in myself."

The next day it was bright, beautiful weather; the sun shone on all the green trees. The mother duck went down to the canal with all her family. Splash! She jumped into the water. "Quack! quack!" she said, and one duckling after another plunged in. The water closed over their heads, but they came up in an instant, and swam; their legs went of themselves, and they were all in the water. The ugly gray duckling swam with them.

"No, it's not a turkey," said the mother, "look how well it can use its legs, and how straight it holds itself. It is my own child! On the whole it's quite pretty, if one looks at it rightly. Quack! quack! Come with me, and I'll lead you out into the great world, and present you in the duck yard; but keep close to me, so that no one may tread on you; and take care of the cats!"

And so they came into the duck yard. There was a terrible riot going on in there, for two families were quarreling about an eel's head, and the cat got it after all.

"See, that's how it goes in the world!" said the mother duck;

Can It Be a Turkey Chick?

and she whetted her beak, for she too wanted the eel's head. "Only use your legs," she said. "See that you all bustle about, and bow your heads before the old duck yonder. She's the grandest of all here; she's of royal blood — that's why she's so fat; and d'ye see? She has a red rag round her leg; that's something particularly fine, and the greatest distinction a duck can enjoy; it signifies that one does not want to lose her, and that she's to be known by animals and by men, too. Shake yourselves, don't turn in your toes; a well-brought-up duck turns its toes quite out, just like — so! Now bend your necks and say 'Quack!'"

And they did so: but the other ducks round about looked at them, and said quite boldly — "Look there! Now we're to have these hanging on, as if there were not enough of us already! And how that duckling yonder looks; we won't stand that!" And one duck flew up at it, and bit it in the neck.

"Let it alone," said the mother; "it does no harm to anyone."

"Yes, but it's too large and peculiar," said the duck who had bitten it; "and therefore it must be put down."

"Those are pretty children that the mother has there," said the old duck with the rag round her leg. "They're all pretty but that one; that was rather unlucky. I wish she could bear it over again."

"That cannot be done, my lady," replied the mother duck. "It is not pretty, but it has a really good disposition, and swims as well as any other; yes, I may even say, it swims better. I think it will

grow up pretty, and become smaller in time; it has lain too long in the egg, and therefore is not properly shaped." And then she pinched it in the neck, and smoothed its feathers. "Moreover it is a drake," she said. "I think he will be very strong: he makes his way already."

"The other ducklings are graceful enough," said the old duck. "Make yourself at home, and if you find an eel's head, you may bring it to me."

And now they were at home. But the poor duckling which had crept last out of the egg, and looked so ugly, was bitten and pushed and jeered, as much by the ducks as by the chickens.

"It is too big!" they all said. And the turkey-cock, who had been born with spurs, and therefore thought himself an emperor, blew himself up like a ship in full sail, and bore straight down upon it; then he gobbled and grew quite red in the face. The poor duckling did not know where it should stand or walk; it was quite melancholy because it looked ugly, and was the butt of the whole duck yard.

So it went on the first day, and afterwards it became worse and worse. The poor duckling was hunted about by everyone; even its brothers and sisters were quite angry with it, and said, "If the cat would only catch you, you ugly creature!" And the mother said, "If you were only far away!" and the ducks bit it, and the chickens beat it, and the girl who had to feed the poultry kicked at it with her foot.

It Became Worse and Worse.

The Ugly Duckling

Then it ran and flew over the fence, and the little birds in the bushes flew up in fear.

"That is because I am so ugly!" thought the duckling. It shut its eyes, but flew on farther; and so it came out into the great moor, where the wild ducks lived. Here it lay the whole night long, and it was weary and downcast.

Toward morning the wild ducks flew up, and looked at their new companion.

"What sort of a one are you?" they asked, and the duckling turned in every direction, and bowed as well as it could. "You are remarkably ugly!" said the wild ducks. "But that is nothing to us."

Poor thing! It only hoped to obtain leave to lie among the reeds and drink some of the swamp water.

Thus it lay two whole days; then there came two wild ganders. It was not long since each had crept out of an egg, and that's why they were so saucy.

"Listen, comrade," said one of them. "You're so ugly that I like you. Will you go with us, and become a bird of passage? Near here, in another moor, there are a few sweet lovely wild geese, all unmarried, and all able to say, 'Rap.' You've a chance of making your fortune, ugly as you are."

"Piff! paff!" resounded through the air; and the two ganders fell down dead in the swamp, and the water became blood red. "Piff! paff!" it sounded again, and the whole flock of wild geese rose up from the reeds. A great hunt was going on. The sportsmen

The Wild Ducks Flew Up.

were all round the moor, some even sitting in the trees. Blue smoke rose up among the trees, and wafted across the water; the hunting dogs came into the swamp, and bent the rushes and reeds.

That frightened the poor duckling! It turned its head under its wing; but at that moment a frightful dog stood close by. His tongue hung out of his mouth, and his eyes gleamed; he thrust out his nose close to the duckling, showed his sharp teeth and away he went, without touching it.

"Oh, thank heaven!" said the duckling. "I am so ugly even a dog does not like me!"

It lay quiet, while gun after gun fired. Late in the day, all was still; the poor duckling did not dare rise, but waited several hours before it hastened out of the moor as fast as it could. It ran on and on, but there was such a raging storm that it was difficult to get anywhere.

The duck came to a miserable little hut, so dilapidated that it did not itself know on which side to fall; that's why it stood. The storm raged around the duckling so that the poor creature had to sit down, to stand it; the wind blew worse and worse. The duckling saw that the hinges of the door had given way, and the door hung so that the duckling could slip through the crack and into the room.

Here lived a woman, with cat and hen. And the cat, whom she called Flixx, could arch his back and purr, and give out sparks; but for that one had to stroke his fur the wrong way. The hen had

Frightful Dog Stood Close By.

short legs, and she was called Little Biddie; she laid good eggs, and the woman loved her well.

In the morning the strange duckling was spotted at once, causing the cat to purr and the hen to cluck.

"What's this?" said the woman. She thought the duckling was a fine catch. "This one is a prize! I hope to have duck's eggs."

The duckling was on trial for three weeks; but no eggs came. The cat was master of the house, and the hen the lady, and they always said, "We and the world!" for they thought they were half the world, and the better half by far. The duckling might have a different opinion, but the hen would not permit that.

"Can you lay eggs?" she asked.

"No."

"Then hold your tongue!"

And the cat said, "Can you curve your back, or give out sparks?"

"No," said the duckling, who sat sadly in a corner.

But when the fresh air and warm sunshine streamed in, it was seized with a strong longing to swim, and could not help telling the hen about it.

"What can you be thinking?" cried the hen. "You have nothing to do, that's why you dream of things. Lay eggs, purr, or do something useful and it will pass."

"But to swim on the water," said the duckling wistfully, "to let it flow over one's head, and to dive to the bottom."

"I fancy you must have gone crazy," said the hen.

The Cat Was Master; the Hen the Lady.

THE UGLY DUCKLING

"You don't understand me," said the duckling. "I think I will go out into the wide world."

"Yes, do," replied the hen.

So the duckling went. It swam and dove, but it was snubbed by everyone because of its looks.

Soon it was autumn. The leaves turned gold and red and brown; the wind caught them about, and the air was very cold. The clouds hung heavy with hail and snow. The poor little duckling watched one evening as there came a flock of great, handsome birds, white, with long, flexible necks: swans.

They spread their great wings, and flew away from that cold region to warmer lands, to fair open lakes. They mounted high and the ugly duckling felt strange as it watched them. It turned in the water like a wheel, stretched its neck toward them, and uttered strange cries, loud and longing.

Then it could see them no longer and it dived down and when it came up again, it was quite sad. It knew not those birds, nor whither they flew; but it loved them more than it had ever thought to have loved any one.

The winter grew very cold. The duckling would swim about in the water, but every night the hole in which it swam became smaller. It froze so hard that the icy covering crackled, and the duckling used its legs continually to keep the hole from entirely freezing. At last it was too exhausted, and lay quite still, and froze into the ice.

There Came a Flock of Great, Handsome Birds.

THE UGLY DUCKLING

The next morning a peasant passing by saw what had happened. He broke the ice and carried the duckling home. Then it came to life again. The children wanted to play, but the duckling thought they wanted to hurt it, and in its terror the poor creature slipped out into the snow where it lay exhausted.

It lay among the reeds until the sun began to shine and it was beautiful spring once again.

All at once the duckling could flap its wings, and more strongly than before, and before it knew how it happened, it found itself in a great garden, where the willows bent their long green branches down to the stream.

From the thicket there came three white swans; they rustled their wings, and swam on the water. The duckling remembered the splendid creatures, and felt a peculiar sadness.

"I will fly to them and they will beat me, because I dare to come near them. Better am I to be killed by *them* than by ducks, and fowls, and pushed about by the girl who cares for the poultry yard, and to suffer in winter!"

It flew out into the water, and swam toward the beautiful swans who looked at it, and came sailing with outspread wings. "Kill me!" said the poor creature, and bent its head down upon the water, expecting its death.

But what it saw in the clear water was its own image; and no longer was it a clumsy bird, ugly and hateful to look at, but a swan!

The Duckling Could Flap Its Wings Again.

THE UGLY DUCKLING

It felt quite glad now as the great swans swam around it, and stroked it.

In the garden little children threw bread and corn seeds into the water, and cried, "There is a new one!" and they shouted joyously, "Yes, a new one has arrived!" They clapped their hands and ran to their parents; now bread and cake were thrown into the water: "The new one is the most beautiful of all! So young and handsome!" they said, and the old swans bowed to him.

He felt quite ashamed, his head under his wings, and did not know what to do, he was so happy. He had been persecuted; now he heard them saying he was most beautiful of all the birds. Even the willow bent its branches into the water before him, and the sun shone warm and mild. Then he lifted his slender neck, and cried rejoicingly from the depths of his heart, "I never dreamed of so much happiness when I was the ugly duckling!"

"The Most Beautiful of All!"

A Fiery Dragon Came Flying Through the Air.

THE · DRAGON · AND · HIS · GRANDMOTHER

T here was once a great war, and the King had a great many soldiers, but he gave them so little pay that they could not live on it. Then three of them took counsel together and determined to desert.

One of them said to the others, "If we are caught, we shall be hanged on the gallows; how shall we get out of it?"

Another said, "Do you see that large cornfield there? If we were to hide ourselves in that, no one could find us. The army cannot come into it, and tomorrow it is to march on."

They crept into the corn, but the army did not march on and remained encamped close around them. They sat for two days and two nights in the corn, and grew so hungry that they nearly died; but if they were to venture out, it was certain death.

They said at last, "What use was it our deserting? We must perish here miserably."

Whilst they were speaking a fiery Dragon came flying through the air. It hovered near them, and asked why they were hidden there.

The Dragon and his Grandmother

They answered, "We are three soldiers, and have deserted because our pay was so small. Now if we remain here we shall die of hunger, and if we move out we shall be strung up on the gallows."

"If you will serve me for seven years," said the Dragon, "I will lead you through the midst of the army so that no one shall catch you."

"We have no choice, and must take your offer," said they.

Then the dragon seized them in his claws, took them through the air over the army, and set them down on the earth a long way from it.

He gave them a little whip, saying, "Whip and slash with this, and as much money as you want will jump up before you. You can then live as great lords, keep horses, and drive about in carriages. But after seven years you are mine." Then he put a book before them, which he made all three of them sign. "I will then give you a riddle," he said; "if you guess it, you shall be free and out of my power." The dragon then flew away, and they journeyed on with their little whip.

They had as much money as they wanted, wore grand clothes, and made their way into the world. Wherever they went they lived in merrymaking and splendor, drove about with horses and carriages, ate and drank, but did nothing really wrong.

The time passed quickly away, and when the seven years were nearly ended, two of them grew terribly anxious and frightened, but the third made light of it, saying, "Don't be afraid, brothers, I wasn't born yesterday; I will guess the riddle."

The Dragon Seized Them in His Claws.

They went into a field, sat down, and the two pulled long faces. An old woman passed by, and asked them why they were so sad. "Alas! What have you to do with it? You cannot help us."

"Who knows?" she answered. "Only confide your trouble in me."

They told her that they had become the servants of the Dragon for seven long years, and how he had given them money as plentiful as blackberries; but as they had signed their names they were his, unless when the seven years had passed they could guess a riddle.

The old woman said, "If you would help yourselves, one of you must go into the wood, and there he will come upon a tumble-down building of rocks which looks like a little house. He must go in, and there he will find help."

The two melancholy ones thought, "That won't save us!" and they remained where they were. But the third merry one jumped up and went into the wood till he found the rock hut.

In the hut sat a very old woman, who was the Dragon's grandmother. She asked him how he came, and what was his business there. He told her all that happened, and because she was pleased with him she took compassion on him, and said she would help him.

She lifted up a large stone which lay over the cellar, saying, "Hide yourself there; you can hear all that is spoken in this room. Only sit still and don't stir. When the Dragon comes, I will ask

In the Hut Sat a Very Old Woman.

him what the riddle is, for he tells me everything; then listen carefully what he answers."

At midnight the Dragon flew in, and asked for his supper. His grandmother laid the table, and brought out food and drink till he was satisfied, and they ate and drank together. Then in the course of the conversation she asked him what he had done in the day, and how many souls he had conquered.

"I haven't had much luck today," he said, "but I have a tight hold on three soldiers."

"Indeed! Three soldiers!" said she. "Who cannot escape you?"

"They are mine," answered the Dragon scornfully, "for I shall only give them one riddle which they will never be able to guess."

"What sort of a riddle is it?" she asked.

"I will tell you this. In the sea lies a dead sea-cat — that shall be their roast meat; and the rib of a whale — that shall be their silver spoon; and the hollow foot of a dead horse — that shall be their wineglass."

When the Dragon had gone to bed, his old grandmother pulled up the stone and let out the soldier.

"Did you pay attention to everything?"

"Yes," he replied, "I know it all, and can help myself splendidly."

Then he went out through the window secretly, and in all haste back to his comrades. He told them how the Dragon had been outwitted by his grandmother, and how he had heard from his own lips the answer to the riddle.

The Dragon Flew In and Asked for His Supper.

They were all delighted and in high spirits, and took out their whip, and cracked so much money that it came jumping up from the ground. When the seven years had quite gone, the Dragon came with his book, and pointing at the signatures, said to the first soldier, "I will take you underground with me; you shall have a meal there. If you can tell me what you will get for your roast meat, you shall be free, and shall also keep the whip."

Then said the first soldier, "In the sea lies a dead sea-cat; that shall be the roast meat."

The Dragon was much annoyed, and hemmed and hawed a good deal, and asked the second, "But what shall be your spoon?"

"The rib of a whale shall be our silver spoon."

The Dragon made a face, and growled again three times, "Hum, hum, hum," and said to the third, "Do you know what your wineglass shall be?"

"An old horse's hoof shall be our wineglass."

Then the Dragon flew away with a loud shriek, and had no more power over them. But the three soldiers took the little whip, whipped as much money as they wanted, and lived happily to their lives' end.

The Money Came Jumping Up from the Ground.

"Spin All Night Till Early Dawn."

RUMPELSTILTSKIN

*T*here was once upon a time a poor miller who had a very
beautiful daughter. Now it happened one day that he had
an audience with the King, and in order to appear a person of some importance he told him that he had a daughter who
could spin straw into gold.

"Now that's a talent worth having," said the King to the
miller; "if your daughter is as clever as you say, bring her to my
palace tomorrow, and I'll put her to the test."

When the girl was brought to him he led her into a room full
of straw, gave her a spinning-wheel and spindle, and said: "Now
set to work and spin all night till early dawn, and if by that time
you haven't spun the straw into gold you shall die." Then he closed
the door behind him and left her alone inside.

So the poor miller's daughter sat down, and didn't know what
in the world she was to do. She hadn't the least idea of how to spin
straw into gold, and became at last so miserable that she began to
cry. Suddenly the door opened, and in stepped a tiny little man

and said: "Good-evening, Miss Miller-maid; why are you crying so bitterly?"

"Oh!" answered the girl, "I have to spin straw into gold, and haven't a notion how it's done."

"What will you give me if I spin it for you?" asked the manikin.

"My necklace," replied the girl.

The little man took the necklace, sat himself down at the wheel, and whir, whir, whir, the wheel went round three times, and the bobbin was full. Then he put on another, and whir, whir, whir, the wheel went round three times, and the second too was full; and so it went on till the morning, when all the straw was spun away, and all the bobbins were full of gold.

As soon as the sun rose the King came, and when he perceived the gold he was astonished and delighted, but his heart only yearned more than ever after the precious metal.

He had the miller's daughter put into another room full of straw, much bigger than the first, and bade her, if she valued her life, spin it all into gold before the following morning.

The girl didn't know what to do, and began to cry; then the door opened as before, and the tiny little man appeared and said: "What'll you give me if I spin the straw into gold for you?"

"The ring from my finger," answered the girl.

The manikin took the ring, and whir! round went the spinning-wheel again, and when morning broke he had spun all the

"What Will You Give Me?"

straw into glittering gold.

The King was pleased beyond measure at the sight, but his greed for gold was still not satisfied, and he had the miller's daughter brought into a yet bigger room full of straw, and said: "You must spin all this away in the night; but if you succeed this time you shall become my wife."

"She's only a miller's daughter, it's true," he thought; "but I could not find a richer wife if I were to search the whole world over."

When the girl was alone the little man appeared for the third time, and said: "What'll you give me if I spin the straw for you once again?"

"I've nothing more to give," answered the girl.

"Then promise me when you are Queen to give me your first child."

"Who knows what may happen before that?" thought the miller's daughter; and besides, she saw no other way out of it, so she promised the manikin what he demanded, and he set to work once more and spun the straw into gold.

When the King came in the morning, and found everything as he had desired, he straightway made her his wife, and the miller's daughter became a Queen.

When a year had passed a beautiful son was born to her, and she thought no more of the little man, till all of a sudden one day he stepped into her room and said: "Now give me what you promised."

"When You Are a Queen . . ."

The Queen was in a great state, and offered the little man all the riches in her kingdom if he would only leave her the child.

But the manikin said: "No, a living creature is dearer to me than all the treasures in the world."

Then the Queen began to cry and sob so bitterly that the little man was sorry for her, and said: "I'll give you three days to guess my name, and if you find it out in that time you may keep your child."

Then the Queen pondered the whole night over all the names she had ever heard, and sent a messenger to scour the land, and to pick up far and near any names he should come across. When the little man arrived on the following day she began with Kasper, Melchior, Belshazzar, and all the other names she knew, in a string, but at each one the manikin called out: "That's not my name."

The next day she sent to inquire the names of all the people in the neighborhood, and had a long list of the most uncommon and extraordinary ones for the little man when he made his appearance.

"Is your name, perhaps, Sheepshanks, Cruickshanks, Spindleshanks?"

But he always replied: "That's not my name."

On the third day the messenger returned and announced: "I have not been able to find any new names, but as I came upon a high hill round the corner of the wood, where the foxes and hares bid each other good night, I saw a little house, and in front of the

A Messenger to Scour the Land

house burned a fire, and round the fire sprang the most grotesque little man, hopping on one leg and crying:

> 'Tomorrow I brew, today I bake,
> And then the child away I'll take;
> For little deems my royal dame
> That Rumpelstiltskin is my name!' "

You may imagine the Queen's delight at hearing the name, and when the little man stepped in shortly afterwards and asked: "Now, my lady Queen, what's my name?" she asked first: "Is your name Conrad?"

"No."

"Is your name Harry?"

"No."

"Is your name, perhaps, Rumpelstiltskin?"

"Some demon has told you that, some demon has told you that!" screamed the little man, and in his rage drove his right foot so far into the ground that it sank in up to his waist; then in a passion he seized the left foot with both hands and tore himself apart.

The King, the Queen, and the little Prince lived happily ever after.

"Some Demon Has Told You That!"

Pinkel Made Himself Useful.

PINKEL · THE · THIEF

*L*ong, long ago there lived a widow who had three sons. The two eldest were grown up, and though they were known to be idle fellows, some of the neighbors had given them work to do on account of the respect in which their mother was held. But at the time this story begins they had both been so careless and idle that their masters declared they would keep them no longer.

So home they went to their mother and youngest brother, of whom they thought little, because he made himself useful about the house, and looked after the hens, and milked the cow. "Pinkel," they called him. And by-and-by "Pinkel" became his name throughout the village.

The two young men thought it was much nicer to live at home and be idle than to be obliged to do a quantity of disagreeable things they did not like; idle they would have stayed till the end of their lives had not the widow lost patience with them and said that since they would not look for work at home they must seek it elsewhere, for she would not have them under her roof any longer.

But she repented bitterly of her words when Pinkel told her that he too was old enough to go out into the world, and that when he had made a fortune he would send for his mother to keep house for him.

The widow wept many tears at parting from her youngest son, but as she saw that his heart was set upon going with his brothers, she did not try to keep him. So the young men started off one morning in high spirits, never doubting that work such as they might be willing to do would be had for the asking, as soon as their little store of money was spent.

But a very few days of wandering opened their eyes. Nobody seemed to want them, or, if they did, the young men declared that they were not able to undertake all that the farmers or millers or woodcutters required of them.

The youngest brother, Pinkel, who was wiser, would gladly have done some of the work that the others refused, but he was small and slight, and no one thought of offering him any. Therefore they went from one place to another, living only on the fruit and nuts they could find in the woods, and getting hungrier every day.

One night, after they had been walking for many hours and were very tired, they came to a large lake with an island in the middle of it. From the island streamed a strong light, by which they

The Young Men Started Off One Morning.

could see everything almost as clear as if the sun had been shining, and they perceived that, lying half hidden in the rushes, was a boat.

"Let us take it and row over to the island, where there must be a house," said the eldest brother; "and perhaps they will give us food and shelter." And they all got in and rowed across in the direction of the light.

As they drew near the island they saw that it came from a golden lantern hanging over the door of a hut, while sweet tinkling music proceeded from some bells attached to the golden horns of a goat which was feeding near the cottage.

The young men's hearts rejoiced as they thought that at last they would be able to rest their weary limbs, and they entered the hut, but were amazed to see an ugly old woman inside, wrapped in a cloak of gold which lighted up the whole house. They looked at each other uneasily as she came forward with her daughter, as they knew by the cloak that this was a famous witch.

"What do you want?" asked she, at the same time signing to her daughter to stir the large pot on the fire.

"We are tired and hungry, and would fain have shelter for the night," answered the eldest brother.

"You cannot get it here," said the witch, "but you will find both food and shelter in the palace on the other side of the lake. Take your boat and go; but leave this boy with me — I can find work for him, though something tells me he is quick and cunning, and will do me ill."

A Cloak of Gold Lighted Up the House.

PINKEL THE THIEF

"What harm can a poor boy like me do a great witch like you?" answered Pinkel. "Let me go, I pray you, with my brothers. I will promise never to hurt you." And at last the witch let him go, and he followed his brothers to the boat.

The way was further than they thought, and it was morning before they reached the palace.

Now, at last, their luck seemed to have turned, for while the two eldest were given places in the King's stables, Pinkel was taken as page to the little Prince. Pinkel was a clever and amusing boy, who saw everything that passed under his eyes, and the King noticed this, and often employed him in his own service, which made his brothers very jealous.

Things went on in this way for some time, and Pinkel every day rose in the royal favor. At length the envy of his brothers became so great that they could bear it no longer, and consulted together how best they might ruin his credit with the King. They did not wish to kill him — though, perhaps, they would not have been sorry if they had heard he was dead — but merely wished to remind him that he was after all only a child, not half so old and wise as they.

Their opportunity soon came. It happened to be the King's custom to visit his stables once a week, so that he might see that his horses were being properly cared for. The next time he entered the stables the two brothers managed to be in the way, and when the King praised the beautiful satin skins of the horses under their

Pinkel Was Page to the Little Prince.

charge, and remarked how different was their condition when his grooms had first come across the lake, the young men at once began to speak of the wonderful light which sprang from the lantern over the hut.

The King, who had a passion for collecting all the rarest things he could find, fell into the trap directly, and inquired where he could get this marvelous lantern.

"Send Pinkel for it, Sire," said they. "It belongs to an old witch, who no doubt came by it in some evil way. But Pinkel has a smooth tongue, and he can get the better of any woman, old or young."

"Then bid him go this very night," cried the King; "and if he brings me the lantern I will make him one of the chief men about my person."

Pinkel was much pleased at the thought of his adventure, and without more ado he borrowed a little boat which lay moored to the shore, and rowed over to the island at once. It was late by the time he arrived, and almost dark, but he knew by the savory smell that reached him that the witch was cooking her supper.

He climbed softly on to the roof, and, peering, watched till the old woman's back was turned, when he quickly drew a handful of salt from his pocket and threw it into the pot. Scarcely had he done this when the witch called her daughter and bade her lift the pot off the fire and put the stew into a dish, as it had been cooking quite long enough and she was hungry.

"Bid Him Go This Very Night."

But no sooner had she tasted it than she put her spoon down, and declared that her daughter must have been meddling with it, and it was impossible to eat anything that was all salt.

"Go down to the spring in the valley, and get some water, that I may prepare a fresh supper," cried she, "for I feel half-starved."

"But, mother," answered the girl, "how can I find the well in this darkness? For you know that the lantern's rays do not reach down there."

"Well, then, take the lantern with you," answered the witch, "for supper I must have, and there is no water that is nearer."

So the girl took her pail in one hand and the golden lantern in the other, and hastened away to the well, followed by Pinkel, who took care to keep out of the way of the rays. When at last she stooped to fill her pail at the well, Pinkel pushed her into it, and snatching up the lantern, hurried back to his boat and rowed off from the shore.

He was already a long distance from the island when the witch, who wondered what had become of her daughter, went to the door to look for her. Close around the hut was thick darkness, but what was that bobbing light that streamed across the water? The witch's heart sank as all at once it flashed upon her what had happened.

"Is that you, Pinkel?" cried she; and the youth answered:

"Yes, dear mother, it is I!"

"Take the Lantern with You."

"And are you not a knave for robbing me?" cried she.

"Truly, dear mother, I am," replied Pinkel, rowing faster than ever, for he was half afraid that the witch might come after him.

But she had no power on the water, and turned angrily into the hut, muttering to herself all the while: "Take care! Take care! A second time you will not escape so easily!"

The sun had not yet risen when Pinkel returned to the palace, and, entering the King's chamber, he held up the lantern so that its rays might fall upon the bed. In an instant the King awoke, and seeing the golden lantern shedding its light upon him, he sprang up, and embraced Pinkel with joy.

"O cunning one," cried he, "what treasure hast thou brought me!" And calling for his attendants he ordered that rooms next to his own should be prepared for Pinkel, and that the youth might enter his presence at any hour. And besides this, he was to have a seat on the council.

It may easily be guessed that all this made the brothers more envious than they were before, and they cast about in their minds afresh how best they might destroy him. At length they remembered the goat with the golden horns and the bells, and they rejoiced; "For," said they, "this time the old woman will be on the watch, and let him be as clever as he likes, the bells on the horns are sure to warn her."

So when, as before, the King came down to the stables and praised the cleverness of their brother, the young men told him of

"You Will Not Escape So Easily!"

that other marvel possessed by the witch, the goat with the golden horns.

From this moment the King never closed his eyes at night for longing after this wonderful creature. He understood something of the danger that there might be in trying to steal it, now that the witch's suspicions were aroused, and he spent hours in making plans for outwitting her. But somehow he never could think of anything that would do, and at last, as the brothers had foreseen, he sent for Pinkel.

"I hear," he said, "that the old witch on the island has a goat with golden horns, from which hang bells that tinkle the sweetest music. That goat I must have! But, tell me, how am I to get it? I would give the third part of my kingdom to anyone who would bring it to me."

"I will fetch it myself," answered Pinkel.

This time it was easier for Pinkel to approach the island unseen, as there was no golden lantern to throw its beams over the water. But, on the other hand, the goat slept inside the hut, and would therefore have to be taken from under the very eyes of the old woman. How was he to do it?

All the way across the lake he thought and thought, till at length a plan came into his head which seemed as if it might do, though he knew it would be very difficult to carry out.

The first thing he did when he reached the shore was to look about for a piece of wood, and when he had found it he hid himself

The Goat with the Golden Horns

close to the hut, till it grew quite dark and near the hour when the witch and her daughter went to bed. Then he crept up and fixed the wood under the door, which opened outwards, in such a manner that the more you tried to shut it the more firmly it stuck.

And this was what happened when the girl went as usual to bolt the door and make all fast for the night:

"What are you doing?" asked the witch, as her daughter kept tugging at the handle.

"There is something the matter with the door; it won't shut," answered she.

"Well, leave it alone; there is nobody to hurt us," said the witch, who was very sleepy; and the girl did as she was bid, and went to bed. Very soon they both were heard snoring, and Pinkel knew that his time was come.

Slipping off his shoes, he stole into the hut on tiptoe, and taking from his pocket some food of which the goat was particularly fond, he laid it under his nose.

Then, while the animal was eating it, he stuffed each golden bell with wool which he had also brought with him, stopping every minute to listen, lest the witch should awaken, and he should find himself changed into some dreadful bird or beast. But the snoring still continued, and he went on with his work as quickly as he could.

When the last bell was done he drew another handful of food out of his pocket, and held it out to the goat, which instantly rose

He Fixed the Wood Under the Door.

to its feet and followed Pinkel, who backed slowly to the door, and directly when he got outside he seized the goat in his arms and ran down to the place where he had moored his boat.

As soon as he had reached the middle of the lake, Pinkel took the wool out of the bells, which began to tinkle loudly. Their sound awoke the witch, who cried out as before:

"Is that you, Pinkel?"

"Yes, dear mother, it is I," said Pinkel.

"Have you stolen my golden goat?" asked she.

"Yes, dear mother, I have," answered Pinkel.

"Are you not a knave, Pinkel?"

"Yes, dear mother, I am," he replied. And the old witch shouted in a rage:

"Ah! Beware how you come hither again, for next time you shall not escape me!"

But Pinkel only laughed and rowed on.

The King was so delighted with the goat that he always kept it by his side, night and day; and, as he had promised, Pinkel was made ruler over the third part of the kingdom. As may be supposed, the brothers were more furious than ever, and grew quite thin with rage.

"How can we get rid of him?" said one to the other. And at length they remembered the golden cloak.

"He will need to be clever if he is to steal that!" they cried with a chuckle. And when next the King came to see his horses,

"Is That You, Pinkel?"

the brothers began to speak of Pinkel and his marvelous cunning, and how he had contrived to steal the lantern and the goat, which nobody else would have been able to do.

"But as he was there, it is a pity he could not have brought away the golden cloak," added they.

"The golden cloak! What is that?" asked the King.

The young men described its beauties in such glowing words that the King declared he should never know a day's happiness till he had wrapped the cloak round his own shoulders.

"And," added he, "the man who brings it to me shall wed my daughter, and shall inherit my throne."

"None can get it save Pinkel," said they; for they did not imagine that the witch, after two warnings, could allow their brother to escape a third time. So Pinkel was sent for, and with a glad heart he set out.

He passed many hours inventing first one plan and then another, till he had a scheme ready which he thought might prove successful.

Thrusting a large bag inside his coat, he pushed off from the shore, taking care this time to reach the island in daylight. Having made his boat fast to a tree, he walked up to the hut, hanging his head, and putting on a face that was both sorrowful and ashamed.

"Is that you, Pinkel?" asked the witch when she saw him, her eyes gleaming savagely.

"Yes, dear mother, it is I," answered Pinkel.

"The Golden Cloak! What Is That?"

"So you have dared, after all you have done, to put yourself in my power!" cried she. "Well, you shan't escape me this time!" And she took down a large knife and began to sharpen it.

"Oh! Dear mother, spare me!" shrieked Pinkel, falling on his knees, and looking wildly about him.

"Spare you, indeed, you thief! Where are my lantern and my goat? No! No! There is only one fate for robbers!" And she brandished the knife in the air so that it glittered in the firelight.

"Then, if I must die," said Pinkel, who by this time was getting really rather frightened, "let me at least choose the manner of my death. I am very hungry, for I have had nothing to eat all day. Put some poison, if you like, into the porridge, but at least let me have a good meal before I die."

"That is not a bad idea," answered the woman; "as long as you do die, it is all one to me." And ladling out a large bowl of porridge, she stirred some poisonous herbs into it, and set about some work that had to be done. Then Pinkel hastily poured all the contents of the bowl into his bag, and made a great noise with his spoon, as if he was scraping up the last morsel.

"Poisoned or not, the porridge is excellent. I have eaten it, every scrap; do give me some more," said Pinkel, turning towards her.

"Well, you have a fine appetite, young man," answered the witch; "however, it is the last time you will ever eat it, so I will give you another bowlful." And rubbing in the poisonous herbs,

She Took Down a Large Knife.

she poured him out half of what remained, and then went to the window to call her cat.

In an instant Pinkel again emptied the porridge into the bag, and the next minute he rolled on the floor, twisting himself about as if in agony, uttering loud groans the while. Suddenly he grew silent and lay still.

"Ah! I thought a second dose of that poison would be too much for you," said the witch, looking at him. "I warned you what would happen if you came back. I wish that all thieves were as dead as you! But why does not my lazy girl bring the wood I sent her for? It will soon be too dark for her to find her way. I suppose I must go and search for her. What a trouble girls are!"

And she went to the door to see if there were any signs of her daughter. But nothing could be seen of her, as heavy rain was falling.

"It is no night for my cloak," she muttered; "it would be covered with mud by the time I got back." So she took it off her shoulders and hung it carefully up in a cupboard in the room. After that she put on her clogs and started to seek her daughter.

Directly after the last sound of the clogs had ceased, Pinkel jumped up and took down the cloak, and rowed off as fast as he could.

He had not gone far when a puff of wind unfolded the cloak, and its brightness shed gleams across the water. The witch, who was just entering the forest, turned round at that moment and saw the golden rays.

Pinkel Jumped Up and Took the Cloak.

She forgot all about her daughter, and ran down to the shore, screaming with rage at being outwitted a third time.

"Is that you, Pinkel?" cried she.

"Yes, dear mother, it is I."

"Have you taken my gold cloak?"

"Yes, dear mother, I have."

"Are you not a great knave?"

"Yes, truly dear mother, I am."

And so indeed he was!

But, all the same, he carried the cloak to the King's palace, and in return he received the hand of the King's daughter in marriage. People said that it was the bride who ought to have worn the cloak at her wedding feast; but the King was so pleased with it that he would not part from it; and to the end of his life was never seen without it.

After his death, Pinkel became King, and let us hope that he gave up his bad and thievish ways, and ruled his subjects well. As for his brothers, he did not punish them, but left them in the stables, where they grumbled all day long.

The King's Daughter in Marriage

They Were Wet Through.

THE · ENCHANTED · WREATH

Once upon a time there lived near a forest a man and his wife and two girls; one girl was the daughter of the man, and the other the daughter of his wife; and the man's daughter was good and beautiful, but the woman's daughter was cross and ugly. However, her mother did not know that, but thought her the most bewitching maiden that ever was seen.

One day the man called to his daughter and bade her come with him into the forest to cut wood. They worked hard all day, but in spite of the chopping they were very cold, for it rained heavily, and when they returned home, they were wet through.

Then, to his vexation, the man found that he had left his ax behind him, and he knew that if it lay all night in the mud it would become rusty and useless. So he said to his wife: "I have dropped my ax in the forest. Bid your daughter go and fetch it, for mine has worked hard all day and is both wet and weary."

But the wife answered:

"If your daughter is wet already, it is all the more reason that *she* should go and get the ax. Besides, she is a great strong girl, and a little rain will not hurt her, while *my* daughter would be sure to catch a bad cold."

By long experience the man knew there was no good saying any more, and with a sigh he told the poor girl she must return to the forest for the ax.

The walk took some time, for it was very dark, and her shoes often stuck in the mud; but she was brave as well as beautiful and never thought of turning back merely because the path was both difficult and unpleasant. At last, with her dress torn by brambles that she could not see, and her face scratched by the twigs on the trees, she reached the spot where she and her father had been cutting in the morning, and found the ax in the place he had left it.

To her surprise, three little doves were sitting on the handle, all of them looking very sad.

"You poor little things," said the girl, stroking them. "Why do you sit there and get wet? Go and fly home to your nest, it will be much warmer than this; but first eat this bread, which I saved from my dinner, and perhaps you will feel happier. It is my father's ax you are sitting on, and I must take it back as fast as I can, or I shall get a terrible scolding from my stepmother."

She crumbled the bread on the ground, and was pleased to see the doves flutter quite cheerfully towards it. "Good-bye," she said, picking up the ax, and went on her way homewards.

By the time they had finished all the crumbs, the doves felt

Three Little Doves Were Sitting on the Handle.

much better, and were able to fly back to their nest in the top of a tree.

"That is a good girl," said one; "I really was too weak to stretch out a wing before she came. I should like to do something to show how grateful I am."

"Well, let us give her a wreath of flowers that will never fade as long as she wears it," cried another.

"And let the tiniest singing birds in the world sit amongst the flowers," rejoined the third.

"Yes, that will do beautifully," said the first. And when the girl stepped into her cottage a wreath of rosebuds was on her head, and a crowd of little birds were singing unseen.

The father, who was sitting by the fire, thought that, in spite of her muddy clothes, he had never seen his daughter looking so lovely; but the stepmother and the other girl grew wild with envy.

"How absurd to walk about on such a pouring night, dressed up like that," she remarked crossly, and roughly pulled off the wreath as she spoke, to place it on her own daughter. As she did so the roses became withered and brown, and the birds flew out of the window.

"See what a useless thing it is!" cried the stepmother. "And now take your supper and go to bed, for it is near upon midnight."

But though she pretended to despise the wreath, she longed none the less for her daughter to have one like it.

Now it happened that the next evening the father, who had been alone in the forest, came back a second time without his ax.

A Wreath of Rosebuds on Her Head

THE ENCHANTED WREATH

The stepmother's heart was glad when she saw this, and she said quite mildly:

"Why, you have forgotten your ax again, you careless man! But now *your* daughter shall stay at home, and *mine* shall go and bring it back;" and throwing a cloak over the girl's shoulders, she bade her hasten to the forest.

With a very ill grace the damsel set forth, grumbling to herself as she went; for though she wished for the wreath, she did not at all want the trouble of getting it.

By the time she reached the spot where her stepfather had been cutting the wood, the girl was in a very bad temper indeed, and when she caught sight of the ax, there were the three little doves, with drooping heads and soiled, bedraggled feathers, sitting on the handle.

"You dirty creatures," cried she, "get away at once, or I will throw stones at you." And the doves spread their wings in a fright and flew up to the very tip of a tree, their bodies shaking with anger.

"What shall we do to revenge ourselves on her?" asked the smallest of the doves, "we were never treated like that before."

"Never," said the biggest dove. "We must find some way of paying her back in her own coin!"

"I know," answered the middle dove; "she shall never be able to say anything but 'dirty creatures' to the end of her life."

"Oh, how clever of you! That will do beautifully," exclaimed

"Mine Shall Go and Bring It Back."

the other two. And they flapped their wings and clucked so loud with delight, and made such a noise, that they woke up all the birds in the trees close by.

"What in the world is the matter?" asked the birds sleepily.

"That is *our* secret," said the doves.

Meanwhile the girl had reached home crosser than ever; as soon as her mother heard her lift the latch of the door, she ran out to hear her adventures. "Well, did you get the wreath?" cried she.

"Dirty creatures!" answered her daughter.

"Don't speak to me like that! What ever do you mean?" asked the mother.

"Dirty creatures!" repeated the daughter, and nothing else could she say.

Then the woman saw that something evil had befallen her, and turned in her rage to her stepdaughter.

"*You* are at the bottom of this, I know," she cried; and as the father was out of the way she took a stick and beat the girl till she went to bed sobbing.

If the poor girl's life had been miserable before, it was ten times worse now, for the moment her father's back was turned, the others teased and tormented her from morning till night; and their fury was increased by the sight of the wreath, which the doves had placed again on her head.

Things went on like this for some weeks, when, one day, as the King's son was riding through the forest, he heard some

"Dirty Creatures!"

strange birds singing more sweetly than birds had ever sung before. He tied his horse to a tree, and followed where the sound led him, and, to his surprise, he saw before him a beautiful girl chopping wood, with a wreath of pink rose-buds, out of which the singing came.

Standing in the shelter of a tree, he watched her a long while, and then, hat in hand, he went up and spoke to her. "Fair maiden, who are you, and who gave you that wreath of singing roses?" asked he, for the birds were so tiny that till you looked closely you never saw them.

"I live in a hut on the edge of the forest," she answered, blushing, for she had never spoken to a Prince before. "And as to the wreath, I know not how it came, unless it may be the gift of some doves whom I fed when they were starving."

The Prince was delighted with this answer, which showed the goodness of the girl's heart, and besides he had fallen in love with her beauty, and would not be content till she promised to return with him to the palace, and become his bride.

The old King was disappointed at his son's choice of a wife, as he wished him to marry a neighboring Princess; but as from his birth the Prince had always done exactly as he liked, nothing was said and a splendid wedding feast was got ready.

The day after her marriage the bride sent a messenger bearing handsome presents to her father, and telling him of the good fortune which had befallen her. As may be imagined, the step-

She Had Never Spoken to a Prince Before.

mother and her daughter were so filled with envy that they grew quite ill, and had to take to their beds, and nobody would have been sorry if they had never got up again; but that did not happen.

At length, they began to feel better, for the mother invented a plan by which she could be revenged on the girl who had never done her any harm.

Her plan was this: In the town where she had lived before she was married there was an old witch, who had more skill in magic than any other witch she knew. To this witch she would go and beg her to make her a mask with the face of her stepdaughter, and when she had the mask the rest would be easy.

She told her daughter what she meant to do and although the daughter could only say "dirty creatures" in answer, she nodded and smiled and looked well pleased.

Everything fell out exactly as the woman had hoped. By the aid of her magic mirror, the witch beheld the new Princess walking in her gardens in a dress of green silk, and in a few minutes had produced a mask so like her that very few people could have told the difference.

However, she counseled the woman that when her daughter first wore it — for that, of course, was what she intended her to do — she had better pretend that she had a toothache, and cover her head with a lace veil. The woman thanked her and paid her well, and returned to her hut, carrying the mask under her cloak.

In a few days she heard that a great hunt was planned, and the

By the Aid of Her Magic Mirror

Prince would leave the palace very early in the morning, so that his wife would be alone all day. This was a chance not to be missed, and taking her daughter with her, she went up to the palace, where she had never been before.

The Princess was too happy in her new home to remember all that she had suffered in the old one, and she welcomed them both gladly, and gave them quantities of beautiful things to take back with them.

At last she took them down to the shore to see a pleasure boat which her husband had made for her; and here, the woman seizing her opportunity, stole softly behind the girl and pushed her off the rock on which she was standing, into the deep water, where she instantly sank to the bottom.

She fastened the mask on her daughter, flung over her shoulders the velvet cloak which the Princess had let fall, and finally arranged a lace veil over her head.

"Rest your cheek on your hand, as if you were in pain, when the Prince returns," said the mother; "and be careful not to speak, whatever you do. I will go back to the witch and see if she cannot take off the spell laid on you by those horrible birds. Ah! Why did I not think of it before!"

No sooner had the Prince entered the palace than he hastened to the Princess's apartments, where he found her lying on a sofa apparently in great pain.

"My dearest wife, what is the matter with you?" he cried,

She Pushed Her Off the Rock.

kneeling down beside her, and trying to take her hand; but she snatched it away, and pointing to her cheek murmured something he could not catch.

"What is it? Tell me! Is the pain bad? When did it begin? Shall I send for your ladies to bathe the place?" asked the Prince, pouring out these and a dozen other questions, to which the girl only shook her head.

"But I can't leave you like this," he continued, starting up. "I must summon all the court physicians to apply soothing balms to the sore place." And as he spoke, he sprang to his feet to go in search of them.

This so frightened the pretended wife, who knew that if the physicians once came near her the trick would at once be discovered, that she forgot her mother's counsel not to speak, and forgot even the spell that had been laid upon her, and catching hold of the Prince's tunic, she cried in tones of entreaty: "Dirty creatures!"

The young man stopped, not able to believe his ears, but supposed that pain had made the Princess cross, as pain sometimes does. However, he guessed somehow that she wished to be left alone, so he only said:

"Well, I dare say a little sleep will do you good, if you can manage to get it, and that you will wake up better tomorrow."

Now, that night happened to be very hot and airless, and the Prince, after vainly trying to rest, went to the window. Suddenly he beheld in the moonlight a form, with a wreath of roses on her

Her Trick Would at Once Be Discovered.

head, rise out of the sea below him and step on to the sands, holding out her arms towards the palace.

"That maiden is strangely like my wife," thought he; "I must see her closer." And he hastened down to the water. But when he got there, the Princess, for she indeed it was, had disappeared completely, and he began to wonder if his eyes had deceived him.

The next morning he went to the false bride's room, but her ladies told him she would neither speak nor get up, though she ate everything they set before her. The Prince was sorely perplexed as to what could be the matter with her, for naturally he could not guess that she was expecting her mother to return every moment, and to remove the spell the doves had laid upon her, and meanwhile was afraid to speak lest she should betray herself.

At length he made up his mind to summon all the court physicians. He did not tell her what he was going to do, lest it should make her worse, but he went himself and begged the four learned men attached to the King's person to follow him to the Princess's apartments.

Unfortunately for her, as they entered, the Princess was so enraged at the sight of them that she forgot all about the doves, and shrieked out: "Dirty creatures! Dirty creatures!" which so offended the physicians that they left the room at once, and nothing that the Prince could say would prevail on them to remain.

He tried to persuade his wife to send them a message that she was sorry for her rudeness, but not a word would she say.

He Beheld a Form in the Moonlight

Late that evening, when he had performed all the tiresome duties which fall to the lot of every Prince, the young man was leaning out of his window, refreshing himself with the cool breezes that blew off the sea. His thoughts went back to the scene of the morning, and he wondered if, after all, he had not made a great mistake in marrying a low-born wife, however beautiful she might be.

How could he have imagined that the quiet, gentle girl who had been so charming a companion to him during the first days of their marriage, could have become in a day the rude, sulky woman, who could not control her temper even to benefit herself?

One thing was clear, if she did not change her conduct very shortly he would have to send her away from court.

He was thinking these thoughts, when his eyes fell on the sea beneath him, and there, as before, was the figure that so closely resembled his wife, standing with her feet in the water, holding out her arms to him.

"Wait for me! Wait for me! Wait for me!" he cried, not even knowing he was speaking. But when he reached the shore there was nothing to be seen but the shadows cast by the moonlight.

A state ceremonial in a city some distance off caused the Prince to ride away at daybreak, and he left without seeing his wife again.

"Perhaps she may have come to her senses by tomorrow," said he to himself; "and, anyhow, if I am going to send her back to her

The Prince Rode Away at Daybreak.

father, it might be better if we did not meet in the meantime."
Then he put the matter from his mind, and kept his thought on
the duty that lay before him.

It was nearly midnight before he returned to the palace, but,
instead of entering, he went down to the shore and hid behind a
rock. He had scarcely done so when the girl came out of the sea,
and stretched out her arms towards his window. In an instant the
Prince had seized her hand, and though she made a frightened
struggle to reach the water — for she in her turn had a spell laid
upon her — he held her fast.

"You are my own wife, and I shall never let you go!" he said.
But the words were hardly out of his mouth when he found that it
was a hare that he was holding by the paw. Then the hare changed
into a fish, and the fish into a bird, and the bird into a slimy wrig-
gling snake. This time the prince's hand nearly opened of itself,
but with a strong effort he kept his fingers shut, and drawing his
sword, cut off its head, and the spell was broken. The girl stood
before him as he had first seen her, the wreath upon her head and
the birds singing for joy.

The very next morning the stepmother arrived at the palace
with an ointment that the old witch had given her to place upon
her daughter's tongue, which would break the dove's spell, if the
rightful bride had really been drowned in the sea; if not, then it
would be useless.

The mother assured her that she had seen her stepdaughter

"I Shall Never Let You Go!"

sink, and that there was no fear that she would ever come up again; but, to make all quite safe, the old woman might bewitch the girl; and so she did.

After that the wicked stepmother traveled all through the night to get to the palace as soon as possible, and made her way straight into her daughter's room. "I have got it! I have got it!" she cried triumphantly, and laid the ointment on her daughter's tongue. "*Now* what do you say?" she asked proudly.

"Dirty creatures! Dirty creatures!" answered the daughter; and the mother wrung her hands and wept, as she knew that all her plans had failed.

At this moment the Prince entered with his real wife. "You both deserve death," he said, "and if it were left to me, you should have it. But the Princess has begged me to spare your lives, so you will be put into a ship and carried off to a desert island, where you will stay till you die."

Then the ship was made ready and the wicked woman and her daughter were placed in it, and it sailed away, and no more was heard of them. But the Prince and his wife lived together long and happily, and ruled their people well.

The Prince and His Wife Lived Long and Well.

From the Four Corners of the World

PRINCESS · MAYBLOSSOM

O nce upon a time there lived a King and Queen whose children had all died, first one and then another, until at last only one little daughter remained, and the Queen was at her wits' end to know where to find a really good nurse who would take care of her, and bring her up.

A herald was sent who blew a trumpet at every street corner, and commanded all the best nurses to appear before the Queen, that she might choose one for the little Princess.

So on the appointed day the whole palace was crowded with nurses, who came from the four corners of the world to offer themselves, until the Queen declared that if she was ever to see the half of them, they must be brought out to her, one by one, as she sat in a shady wood near the palace.

This was accordingly done, and the nurses, after they had made their curtsey to the King and Queen, ranged themselves in a line before her that she might choose. Most of them were fair and fat and charming, but there was one who was ugly, and spoke a strange language which nobody could understand.

The Queen wondered how she dared offer herself, and she was told to go away, as she certainly would not do. Upon which she muttered something and passed on, but hid herself in a hollow tree, from which she could see all that happened.

The Queen, without giving her another thought, chose a pretty rose-faced nurse, but no sooner was her choice made than a snake, which was hidden in the grass, bit that very nurse on her foot, so that she fell down as if dead.

The Queen was very much vexed by this accident, but she soon selected another, who was just stepping forward when an eagle flew by and dropped a large tortoise upon her head, which was cracked in pieces like an egg shell.

At this the Queen was much horrified; nevertheless, she chose a third time, but with no better fortune, for the nurse, moving quickly, ran into the branch of a tree and blinded herself with a thorn.

Then the Queen in dismay cried that there must be some malignant influence at work, and that she would choose no more that day; and she had just risen to return to the palace when she heard peals of malicious laughter behind her, and turning round saw the ugly stranger whom she had dismissed, who was making very merry over the disasters and mocking everyone, but especially the Queen.

This annoyed Her Majesty very much, and she was about to

She Hid Herself in a Hollow Tree.

order that she should be arrested, when the witch — for she was a witch — with two blows from a wand summoned a chariot of fire drawn by winged dragons, and was whirled off through the air uttering threats and cries.

When the King saw this he cried:

"Alas! Now we are ruined indeed, for that was no other than the Fairy Carabosse, who has had a grudge against me ever since I was a boy and put sulphur into her porridge one day for fun."

Then the Queen began to cry.

"If I had only known who it was," she said, "I would have done my best to make friends with her; now I suppose all is lost."

The King was sorry to have frightened her so much, and proposed that they should go and hold a council as to what was best to be done to avert the misfortunes which Carabosse certainly meant to bring upon the little Princess.

So all the counsellors were summoned to the palace, and when they had shut every door and window, and stuffed up every keyhole that they might not be overheard, they talked the affair over, and decided that every fairy for a thousand leagues round should be invited to the christening of the Princess, and that the time of the ceremony should be kept a profound secret, in case the Fairy Carabosse should take it into her head to attend it.

The Queen and her ladies set to work to prepare presents for the fairies who were invited: for each one a blue velvet cloak, a petticoat of apricot satin, a pair of high-heeled shoes, some sharp

Whirled Through the Air

needles, and a pair of golden scissors.

Of all the fairies the Queen knew, only five were able to come on the day appointed, but they began immediately to bestow gifts upon the Princess.

One promised that she should be perfectly beautiful, the second that she should understand anything — no matter what — the first time it was explained to her, the third that she should sing like a nightingale, the fourth that she should succeed in everything she undertook, and the fifth was opening her mouth to speak when a tremendous rumbling was heard in the chimney, and Carabosse, all covered with soot, came rolling down, crying:

"I say that she shall be the unluckiest of the unlucky until she is twenty years old."

Then the Queen and all the fairies began to beg and beseech her to think better of it, and not be so unkind to the poor little Princess, who had never done her any harm. But the ugly old Fairy only grunted and made no answer. So the last Fairy, who had not yet given her gift, tried to mend matters by promising the Princess a long and happy life after the fatal time was over.

At this Carabosse laughed maliciously, and climbed away up the chimney, leaving them all in great consternation, especially the Queen. However, she entertained the fairies splendidly, and gave them beautiful ribbons, of which they are very fond, in addition to the other presents.

When they were going away the oldest Fairy said that they

"Unluckiest of the Unlucky"

were of opinion that it would be best to shut the Princess up in some place, with her waiting-women, so that she might not see anyone else until she was twenty years old.

So the King had a tower built for that purpose. It had no windows, so it was lighted with wax candles, and the only way into it was by an underground passage, which had iron doors only twenty feet apart, and guards were posted everywhere.

The Princess had been named Mayblossom, because she was as fresh and blooming as Spring itself, and she grew up tall and beautiful, and everything she did and said was charming. Every time the King and Queen came to see her they were more delighted with her than before, but though she was weary of the tower, and often begged them to take her away from it, they always refused. The Princess's nurse, who had never left her, sometimes told her about the world outside the tower, and though the Princess had never seen anything for herself, yet she always understood exactly, thanks to the second Fairy's gift.

Often the King said to the Queen:

"We were cleverer than Carabosse after all. Our Mayblossom will be happy in spite of her predictions."

And the Queen laughed until she was tired, at the idea of having outwitted the old Fairy. They had caused the Princess's portrait to be painted and sent to all the neighboring courts, for in four days she would have completed her twentieth year, and it was time to decide whom she should marry.

The King Had a Tower Built.

PRINCESS MAYBLOSSOM

All the town was rejoicing at the thought of the Princess's approaching freedom, and when the news came that King Merlin was sending his ambassador to ask her in marriage for his son, they were still more delighted.

The nurse, who kept the Princess informed of everything that went forward in the town, did not fail to repeat the news that so closely concerned her, and gave such a description of the splendor in which the ambassador Fanfaronade would enter the town, that the Princess was wild to see the procession for herself.

"What an unhappy creature I am," she cried, "to be shut up in this dismal tower as if I had committed some crime! I have never seen the sun, or the stars, or a horse, or a monkey, or a lion, except in pictures, and though the King and Queen tell me I am to be set free when I am twenty, I believe they only say it to keep me amused when they never mean to let me out at all."

And then she began to cry, and her nurse, and the nurse's daughter, and the cradle-rocker, and the nursery-maid, who all loved her dearly, cried too for company, so that nothing could be heard but sobs and sighs. It was a scene of woe.

When the Princess saw that they all pitied her she made up her mind to have her own way. So she declared that she would starve herself to death if they did not find some means of letting her see Fanfaronade's grand entry into the town.

"If you really love me," she said, "you will manage it, somehow or other, and the King and Queen need never know

The Princess Was Wild to See the Procession.

anything about it."

Then the nurse and all the others cried harder than ever, and said everything they could think of to turn the Princess from her idea. But the more they said the more determined she was, and at last they consented to make a tiny hole in the tower on the side that looked towards the city gates.

After scratching and scraping all day and all night, they presently made a hole through which they could, with great diffi-·culty, push a very slender needle, and out of this the Princess looked at the daylight for the first time. She was so dazzled and delighted by what she saw, that there she stayed, never taking her eyes away from the peep-hole for a single minute, until presently the ambassador's procession appeared in sight.

At the head of it rode Fanfaronade himself upon a white horse, which pranced and caracoled to the sound of the trumpets. Nothing could have been more splendid than the ambassador's attire. His coat was nearly hidden under an embroidery of pearls and diamonds, his boots were solid gold, and from his helmet floated scarlet plumes. At the sight of him the Princess lost her wits entirely, and determined that Fanfaronade and nobody else would she marry.

"It is quite impossible," she said, "that his master should be half as handsome and delightful. I am not ambitious, and having spent all my life in this tedious tower, anything — even a house in the country — will seem a delightful change. I am sure that bread

Fanfaronade Himself Upon a White Horse

and water shared with Fanfaronade will please me far better than roast chicken and sweetmeats with anybody else."

And so she went on talk, talk, talking, until her waiting-women wondered where she got it all from. But when they tried to stop her, and suggested that her high rank made it perfectly impossible that she should do any such thing, she would not listen, and ordered them to be silent.

As soon as the ambassador arrived at the palace, the Queen started to fetch her daughter.

All the streets were spread with carpets, and the windows were full of ladies who were waiting to see the Princess, and carried baskets of flowers and sweetmeats to shower upon her as she passed.

They had hardly begun to get the Princess ready when a dwarf arrived, mounted upon an elephant. He came from the five fairies, and brought for the Princess a crown, a scepter, and a robe of golden brocade, with a petticoat marvelously embroidered with butterflies' wings. They also sent a casket of jewels, so splendid that no one had ever seen anything like it before, and the Queen was perfectly dazzled when she opened it.

But the Princess scarcely gave a glance to any of these treasures, for she thought of nothing but Fanfaronade. The Dwarf was rewarded with a gold piece, and decorated with so many ribbons that it was hardly possible to see him at all.

The Princess sent to each of the fairies a new spinning-wheel

Waiting to See the Princess

with a distaff of cedar wood, and the Queen said she must look through her treasures and find something very charming to send them also.

When the Princess was arrayed in all the gorgeous things the Dwarf had brought, she was more beautiful than ever, and as she walked along the streets the people cried: "How pretty she is! How pretty she is!"

The procession consisted of the Queen, the Princess, five dozen other Princesses, her cousins; and ten dozen who came from the neighboring kingdoms; and as they proceeded at a stately pace the sky began to grow dark, then suddenly the thunder growled, and rain and hail fell in torrents.

The Queen put her royal mantle over her head, and all the Princesses did the same with their trains. Mayblossom was just about to follow their example when a terrific croaking, as of an immense army of crows, rooks, ravens, screech-owls, and all birds of ill-omen was heard, and at the same instant a huge owl skimmed up to the Princess, and threw over her a scarf woven of spiders' webs and embroidered with bats' wings.

And then peals of mocking laughter rang through the air, and they knew that this was another of the Fairy Carabosse's unpleasant jokes.

The Queen was terrified at such an evil omen, and tried to pull the black scarf from the Princess's shoulders, but it really seemed as if it must be nailed on, it clung so closely.

A Huge Owl Skimmed Up to the Princess.

"Ah!" cried the Queen, "Can nothing appease this enemy of ours? What good was it that I sent her more than fifty pounds of sweetmeats, and as much again of the best sugar, not to mention two hams? She is as angry as ever."

While she lamented in this way, and everybody was as wet as if they had been dragged through a river, the Princess still thought of nothing but the ambassador, and just at this moment he appeared before her, with the King, and there was a great blowing of trumpets, and all the people shouted louder than ever.

Fanfaronade was not generally at a loss for something to say, but when he saw the Princess, she was so much more beautiful and majestic than he had expected that he could only stammer out a few words, and entirely forgot the harangue which he had been learning for months, and knew well enough to have repeated it in his sleep.

To gain time to remember at least part of it, he made several low bows to the Princess, who on her side dropped half-a-dozen curtseys without stopping to think, and then she said, to relieve his evident embarrassment:

"Sir Ambassador, I am sure that everything you intend to say is charming, since it is you who mean to say it; but let us make haste into the palace, as it is pouring cats and dogs, and the wicked Fairy Carabosse will be amused to see us all stand dripping here. When we are once under shelter we can laugh at her."

Upon this the ambassador found his tongue, and replied

The Ambassador Appeared Before Her.

gallantly that the Fairy had evidently foreseen the flames that would be kindled by the bright eyes of the Princess, and had sent this deluge to extinguish them.

Then he offered his hand to conduct the Princess, and she said softly: "As you could not possibly guess how much I like you, Sir Fanfaronade, I am obliged to tell you plainly that, since I saw you enter the town on your beautiful prancing horse, I have been sorry that you came to speak for another instead of for yourself. So, if you feel as I do, I will marry you instead of your master. Of course I know you are not a Prince, but I shall be just as fond of you as if you were, and we can go and live in some cozy little corner of the world, and be as happy as the days are long."

The ambassador thought he must be dreaming, and could hardly believe what the lovely Princess had said. He dared not answer, but only squeezed the Princess's hand until he really hurt her little finger, but she did not cry out.

When they reached the palace the King kissed his daughter on both cheeks, and said: "My little lambkin, are you willing to marry the great King Merlin's son, as this ambassador has come on his behalf to fetch you?"

"If you please, sire," said the Princess, dropping a curtsey.

"I consent also," said the Queen; "so let the banquet be prepared."

This was done with all speed, and everybody feasted except Mayblossom and Fanfaronade, who looked at one another and

"You Came to Speak for Another."

forgot everything else.

After the banquet came a ball, and after that a ballet, and at last they were all so tired that everyone feel asleep just where he sat. Only the lovers were as wide awake as mice, and the Princess, seeing that there was nothing to fear, said to Fanfaronade:

"Let us be quick and run away, for we shall never have a better chance than this."

Then she took the King's dagger, which was in a diamond sheath, and the Queen's neck-handkerchief, and gave her hand to Fanfaronade, who carried a lantern, and they ran out together into the muddy street and down to the seashore.

Here they got into a little boat in which the poor old boat-man was sleeping, and when he woke up and saw the lovely Princess, with all her diamonds and her spiders'-web scarf, he did not know what to think, and obeyed her instantly when she commanded him to set out.

They could see neither moon nor stars, but in the Queen's neck-handkerchief there was a carbuncle which glowed like fifty torches.

Fanfaronade asked the Princess where she would like to go, but she only answered that she did not care where she went as long as he was with her.

"But, Princess," said he, "I dare not take you back to King Merlin's court. He would think hanging too good for me."

"Oh, in that case," she answered, "we had better go to Squirrel

She Took the King's Dagger and They Ran Out Together.

Island; it is lonely enough, and too far for anyone to follow us there."

So she ordered the old boatman to steer for Squirrel Island.

Meanwhile the day was breaking, and the King and Queen and all the courtiers began to wake up and rub their eyes, and think it was time to finish the preparations for the wedding. And the Queen asked for her neck-handkerchief, that she might look richly dressed for her daughter's ceremony.

Then there was a scurrying hither and thither, and a hunting everywhere: they looked into every place, from the wardrobes to the stoves, and the Queen herself ran about from the garret to the cellar, but the handkerchief was nowhere to be found.

By this time the King had missed his dagger, and the search began all over again. They opened boxes and chests of which the keys had been lost for a hundred years, and found numbers of curious things, but not the dagger, and the King tore his beard, and the Queen tore her hair, for the handkerchief and the dagger were the most valuable things in the kingdom.

When the King saw that the search was hopeless he said:

"Never mind, let us make haste and get the wedding over before anything else is lost." And then he asked where the Princess was. Upon this her nurse came forward and said: "Sire, I have been seeking her these two hours, but she is nowhere to be found."

This was more than the Queen could bear. She gave a shriek of alarm and fainted away, and they had to pour two barrels of eau-

The Handkerchief Was Nowhere to Be Found.

de-cologne over her before she recovered.

When she came to herself everybody was looking for the Princess in the greatest terror and confusion, but as she did not appear, the King said to his page: "Go and find the Ambassador Fanfaronade, who is doubtless asleep in some corner, and tell him the sad news."

So the page hunted hither and thither, but Fanfaronade was no more to be found than the Princess, the dagger, or the neck-handkerchief!

Then the King summoned his counsellors and his guards, and, accompanied by the Queen, went into his great hall. As he had not had time to prepare his speech beforehand, the King ordered that silence should be kept for three hours, and at the end of that time he spoke as follows:

"Listen, great and small! My dear daughter Mayblossom is lost: whether she had been stolen away or has simply disappeared I cannot tell. The Queen's neck-handkerchief and my sword, which are worth their weight in gold, are also missing, and worst of all, the Ambassador Fanfaronade is nowhere to be found. I fear the King, his master, will come to seek him, and accuse us of having made mince-meat of him. I could bear even that if I had any money, but I assure you that the expenses of the wedding have completely ruined me. Advise me, then, my dear subjects, what had I better do to recover my daughter, Fanfaronade, and the other things."

This was the most eloquent speech the King had been known

Silence for Three Hours

to make, and when everybody had done admiring it the Prime Minister made answer:

"Sire, we are all very sorry to see you so sorry. We would give everything we value in the world to take away the cause of your sorrow, but this seems to be another of the tricks of the Fairy Carabosse. The Princess's twenty unlucky years were not quite over, and really, if the truth must be told, I noticed that Fanfaronade and the Princess appeared to admire one another greatly. Perhaps this may give us some clue to the mystery of their disappearance."

Here the Queen interrupted him, saying, "Take care what you say, sir. Believe me, the Princess Mayblossom was far too well brought up to think of falling in love with an ambassador."

At this moment the nurse came forward, and, falling on her knees, confessed how they had made the little needle-hole in the tower, and how the Princess had declared when she saw the ambassador that she would marry him and nobody else.

Then the Queen was very angry, and gave the nurse, and the cradle-rocker, and the nursery-maid, such a scolding that they shook in their shoes.

But the Admiral Cocked-Hat interrupted her, crying: "Let us be off after this good-for-nothing Fanfaronade, for without a doubt he has run away with our Princess."

Then there was a great clapping of hands, and everybody shouted, "By all means let us be after him."

So while some embarked upon the sea, the others ran from

The Nurse Came Forward.

kingdom to kingdom beating drums and blowing trumpets, and wherever a crowd collected they cried:

"Whoever wants a beautiful doll, sweetmeats of all kinds, a little pair of scissors, a golden robe, and a satin cap has only to say where Fanfaronade has hidden the Princess Mayblossom."

But the answer everywhere was, "You must go farther, we have not seen them."

However, those who went by sea were more fortunate, for after sailing about for some time they noticed a light before them which burned at night like a great fire. At first they dared not go near it, not knowing what it might be, but by-and-by it remained stationary over Squirrel Island, for, as you have guessed already, the light was the glowing of the carbuncle.

The Princess and Fanfaronade on landing upon the island had given the boatman a hundred gold pieces, and made him promise solemnly to tell no one where he had taken them; but the first thing that happened was that, as he rowed away, he got into the midst of the fleet, and before he could escape the Admiral had seen him and sent a boat after him.

When he was searched they found the gold pieces in his pocket, and as they were quite new coins, struck in honor of the Princess's wedding, the Admiral felt certain that the boatman must have been paid by the Princess to aid her in her flight. But he would not answer any questions, and pretended to be deaf and dumb.

Then the Admiral said: "Oh! Deaf and dumb is he? Lash him

A Light Like a Great Fire

to the mast and give him a taste of the cat-o'-nine-tails. I don't know anything better than that for curing the deaf and dumb!"

And when the old boatman saw that he was in earnest, he told all he knew about the cavalier and the lady whom he had landed upon Squirrel Island, and the Admiral knew it must be the Princess and Fanfaronade; so he gave the order for the fleet to surround the island.

Meanwhile the Princess Mayblossom, who was by this time terribly sleepy, had found a grassy bank in the shade, and throwing herself down had already fallen asleep into a profound slumber, when Fanfaronade, who happened to be hungry and not sleepy, came and woke her up, saying very crossly:

"Pray, madam, how long do you mean to stay here? I see nothing to eat, and though you may be very charming, the sight of you does not prevent me from famishing."

"What! Fanfaronade," said the Princess, sitting up and rubbing her eyes, "is it possible that when I am here with you you can want anything else? You ought to be thinking all the time how happy you are."

"Happy!" cried he; "Say rather unhappy. I wish with all my heart that you were back in your dark tower again."

"Darling, don't be cross," said the Princess. "I will go and see if I can find some wild fruit for you."

"I wish you might find a wolf to eat you up," growled Fanfaronade.

The Old Boatman Told All He Knew.

The Princess, in great dismay, ran hither and thither all about the wood, tearing her dress, and hurting her pretty hands with the thorns and brambles, but she could find nothing to eat, and at last she had to go back sorrowfully to Fanfaronade.

When he saw that she came empty-handed he got up and left her, grumbling to himself.

The next day they searched again, but with no better success.

"Alas!" said the Princess, "If only I could find something for you to eat, I should not mind being hungry myself."

"No, I should not mind that either," answered Fanfaronade.

"Is it possible," said she, "that you would not care if I died of hunger? Oh, Fanfaronade, you said you loved me!"

"That was when we were in quite another place and I was not hungry," said he. "It makes a great difference in one's ideas to be dying of hunger and thirst on a desert island."

At this the Princess was dreadfully vexed, and she sat down under a white rose bush and began to cry bitterly.

"Happy roses," she thought to herself, "they have only to blossom in the sunshine and be admired, and there is nobody to be unkind to them."

And the tears ran down her cheeks and splashed on to the rose-tree roots. Presently she was surprised to see the whole bush rustling and shaking, and a soft little voice from the prettiest rose-bud said:

"Poor Princess! Look in the trunk of that tree, and you will

The Princess Ran Hither and Thither.

find a honeycomb, but don't be foolish enough to share it with Fanfaronade."

Mayblossom ran to the tree, and sure enough there was the honey. Without losing a moment she ran with it to Fanfaronade, crying gaily:

"See, here is a honeycomb that I have found. I might have eaten it up all by myself, but I had rather share it with you."

But without looking at her or thanking her he snatched the honeycomb out of her hands and ate it all up — every bit, without offering her a morsel. Indeed, when she humbly asked for some he said mockingly that it was too sweet for her, and would spoil her teeth.

Mayblossom, more downcast than ever, went sadly away and sat down under an oak tree, and her tears and sighs were so piteous that the oak fanned her with his rustling leaves, and said:

"Take courage, pretty Princess, all is not lost yet. Take this pitcher of milk and drink it up, and whatever you do, don't leave a drop for Fanfaronade."

The Princess, quite astonished, looked round, and saw a big pitcher full of milk, but before she could raise it to her lips the thought of how thirsty Fanfaronade must be, after eating at least fifteen pounds of honey, made her run back to him and say: "Here is a pitcher of milk; drink some, for you must be thirsty, I am sure; but pray save a little for me, as I am dying of hunger and thirst."

But he seized the pitcher and drank all it contained at a single

"Here Is a Honeycomb I Have Found."

draught, and then broke it to atoms on the nearest stone, saying, with a malicious smile: "As you have not eaten anything you cannot be thirsty."

"Ah!" cried the Princess, "I am well punished for disappointing the King and Queen, and running away with this ambassador, about whom I knew nothing."

And so saying she wandered away into the thickest part of the wood, and sat down under a thorn tree, where a nightingale was singing. Presently she heard him say: "Search under the bush, Princess; you will find some sugar, almonds, and some tarts there. But don't be silly enough to offer Fanfaronade any."

And this time the Princess, who was fainting with hunger, took the nightingale's advice, and ate what she found all by herself. But Fanfaronade, seeing that she had found something good, and was not going to share it with him, ran after her in such a fury that she hastily drew out the Queen's carbuncle, which had the property of rendering people invisible if they were in danger, and when she was safely hidden from him she reproached him gently for his unkindness.

Meanwhile Admiral Cocked-Hat had despatched Jack-the-Chatterer-of-the-Straw-Boots, Courier in Ordinary to the Prime Minister, to tell the King that the Princess and the ambassador had landed on Squirrel Island, but that not knowing the country he had not pursued them, for fear of being captured by concealed enemies. Their Majesties were overjoyed at the news, and the

"You Cannot Be Thirsty."

King sent for a great book, each leaf of which was eight ells long. It was the work of a very clever Fairy, and contained a description of the whole earth. He very soon found that Squirrel Island was uninhabited.

"Go," said he to Jack-the-Chatterer, "tell the Admiral from me to land at once. I am surprised at his not having done so sooner." As soon as this message reached the fleet, every preparation was made for war, and the noise was so great that it reached the ears of the Princess, who at once flew to protect her ambassador. As he was not very brave he accepted her aid gladly.

"You stand behind me," said she, "and I will hold the carbuncle which will make us invisible, and with the King's dagger I can protect you from the enemy."

So when the soldiers landed they could see nothing, but the Princess touched them one after another with the dagger, and they fell insensible upon the sand, so that at last the Admiral, seeing that there was some enchantment, hastily gave orders for a retreat to be sounded, and got his men back into their boats in great confusion.

Fanfaronade, being once more left with the Princess, began to think that if he could get rid of her, and possess himself of the carbuncle and the dagger, he would be able to make his escape.

So as they walked back over the cliffs he gave the Princess a great push, hoping she would fall into the sea; but she stepped aside so quickly that he only succeeded in overbalancing himself,

Every Preparation Was Made for War.

and over he went, and sank to the bottom of the sea like a lump of lead, and was never heard of any more.

While the Princess was still looking after him in horror, her attention was attracted by a rushing noise over her head, and looking up she saw two chariots approaching rapidly from opposite directions.

One was bright and glittering, and drawn by swans and peacocks, while the Fairy who sat in it was beautiful as a sunbeam; but the other was drawn by bats and ravens, and contained a frightful little Dwarf, who was dressed in a snake's skin, and wore a great toad upon her head for a hood.

The chariots met with a frightful crash in mid-air, and the Princess looked on in breathless anxiety while a furious battle took place between the lovely Fairy and her golden lance, and the hideous little Dwarf and her rusty pike. But very soon it was evident that the beauty had the best of it, and the Dwarf turned her bats' heads and flickered away in great confusion.

The Fairy came down to where Mayblossom stood, and said, smiling: "You see, Princess, I have completely routed that malicious old Carabosse. Will you believe it! She actually wanted to claim authority over you forever, because you came out of the tower four days before the twenty years were ended. However, I think I have settled her pretensions, and I hope you will be very happy and enjoy the freedom I have won for you."

The Princess thanked her heartily, and then the Fairy

Two Chariots Approaching

despatched one of her peacocks to her palace to bring a gorgeous robe for Mayblossom, who certainly needed it, for her own was torn to shreds by the thorns and briars. Another peacock was sent to the Admiral to tell him that he could now land in perfect safety, which he at once did, bringing all his men with him, even to Jack-the-Chatterer, who, happening to pass the spit upon which the Admiral's dinner was roasting, snatched it up and brought it with him.

Admiral Cocked-Hat was immensely surprised when he came upon the golden chariot, and still more so to see two lovely ladies walking under the trees a little farther away. When he reached them, of course he recognized the Princess, and he went down on his knees and kissed her hand quite joyfully. Then she presented him to the Fairy, and told him how Carabosse had been finally routed, and he thanked and congratulated the Fairy, who was most gracious to him.

While they were talking, she cried suddenly: "I declare I smell a savory dinner."

"Why yes, Madam, here it is," said Jack-the-Chatterer, holding up the spit, where all the pheasants and partridges were frizzling. "Will Your Highness please to taste any of them?"

"By all means," said the Fairy, "especially as the Princess will certainly be glad of a good meal."

So the Admiral sent back to his ship for everything that was needful, and they feasted merrily under the trees. By the time they

Another Peacock Was Sent to the Admiral.

had finished, the peacock had come back with a robe for the Princess, in which the Fairy arrayed her. It was of green and gold brocade, embroidered with pearls and rubies, and her long golden hair was tied back with strings of diamonds and emeralds, and crowned with flowers.

The Fairy made her mount beside her in the golden chariot, and took her on board the Admiral's ship, where she bade her farewell, sending many messages of friendship to the Queen, and bidding the Princess tell her that she was the fifth Fairy who had attended the christening. Then salutes were fired, the fleet weighed anchor, and very soon they reached the port.

Here the King and Queen were waiting, and they received Mayblossom with such joy and kindness that she could not get a word in edgewise, to say how sorry she was for having run away with such a very poor spirited ambassador. But, after all, it must have been all Carabosse's fault.

Just at this lucky moment who should arrive but King Merlin's son, who had become uneasy at not receiving any news from his ambassador, and so had started out himself with a magnificent escort of a thousand horsemen, and thirty body-guards in gold and scarlet uniforms, to see what could have happened.

As he was a hundred times handsomer and braver than the ambassador, the Princess found she could like him very much. So the wedding was held at once, with so much splendor and rejoicing that all the previous misfortunes were quite forgotten.

King Merlin's Son

Always Smashing, Upsetting, Breaking!

How · Moti · Won · The · War

O nce upon a time there was a youth called Moti, who was very big and strong, but the clumsiest creature you can imagine. So clumsy was he that he was always putting his great feet into the bowls of sweet milk which his mother set out on the floor to cool, always smashing, upsetting, breaking, until at last his father said to him:

"Here, Moti, are fifty silver pieces which are the savings of years; take them and go and make your living or your fortune if you can."

Then Moti started off early one spring morning with his thick staff over his shoulder, singing gaily to himself as he walked along.

In one way and another he got along very well until a hot evening when he came to a certain city where he entered the travelers' serai, or inn, to pass the night. Now a serai is generally just a large square enclosed by a high wall with an open colonnade along the inside all round to accommodate both men and beasts, and with perhaps a few rooms in towers at the corners for those who are too rich or too proud to sleep by their own camels and horses.

Moti, of course, was a country lad and had lived with cattle all his life, and he wasn't rich and he wasn't proud, so he just borrowed a bed from the innkeeper, set it down beside an old buffalo who reminded him of home, and in five minutes was fast asleep.

In the middle of the night he woke, feeling that he had been disturbed, and putting his hand under his pillow found to his horror that his bag of money had been stolen!

He jumped up quietly and began to prowl around to see whether anyone seemed to be awake, but, though he managed to arouse a few men and beasts by falling over them, he walked in the shadow of the archways round the whole serai without coming across a likely thief.

He was just about to give up when he overheard two men whispering, and one laughed softly, and, peering behind a pillar, he saw two Afghan horsedealers counting out his bag of money! Then Moti went back to bed.

In the morning Moti followed the two dealers outside the city to the horsemarket in which their horses were offered for sale. Choosing the best-looking horse amongst them he went up to it and said:

"Is this horse for sale? May I try it?" and, the merchants assenting, he scrambled up on its back, dug in his heels, and off they flew. Now Moti had never been on a horse in his life, and had

His Money Had Been Stolen!

so much to do to hold on with both hands as well as with both legs that the animal went just where it liked, and very soon broke into a break-neck gallop and made straight back to the serai where it had spent the last few nights.

"This will do very well," thought Moti as they whirled in at the entrance. As soon as the horse had arrived at its stable it stopped of its own accord and Moti immediately rolled off; but he jumped up at once, tied the beast up, and called for some breakfast. Presently the dealers appeared, out of breath and furious, and claimed the horse.

"What do you mean?" cried Moti, with his mouth full of rice. "It's my horse; I paid you fifty pieces of silver for it — quite a bargain, I'm sure!"

"Nonsense! It is *our* horse," answered one of the Afghans, beginning to untie the bridle.

"Leave off," shouted Moti, seizing his staff; "if you don't let my horse alone I'll crack your skulls! You thieves! *I* know you! Last night you took my money, so today I took your horse; that's fair enough!"

Now they began to look a little uncomfortable, but Moti seemed so determined to keep the horse that they resolved to appeal to the law, so they went off and laid a complaint before the King that Moti had stolen one of their horses and would not give it up nor pay for it.

Presently a soldier came to summon Moti to the King; and,

"It Is *Our* House!"

when he arrived and made his obeisance, the King began to question him as to why he had galloped off with the horse in this fashion. But Moti declared that he had got the animal in exchange for fifty pieces of silver, whilst the horse merchants vowed that the money they had on them was what they had received for the sale of other horses.

In one way and another the dispute got so confusing that the King (who really thought that Moti had stolen the horse) said at last: "Well, I tell you what I will do. I will lock something into this box before me, and if he guesses what it is, the horse is his, and if he doesn't, then it is yours."

To this Moti agreed, and the King arose and went out alone by a little door at the back of the court, and presently came back clasping something closely wrapped up in a cloth under his robe, slipped it into the little box, locked the box, and set it up where all might see.

"Now," said the King to Moti, "guess!"

It happened that when the King had opened the door behind him, Moti noticed that there was a garden outside: without waiting for the King's return he began to think what could be got out of the garden small enough to be shut in the box.

"Is it likely to be a fruit or a flower? No, not a flower this time, for he clasped it too tight. Then it must be a fruit or a stone. Yet not a stone, because he wouldn't wrap a dirty stone in his nice clean cloth.

"Now," said the King, "Guess!"

"Then it is a fruit! And a fruit without much scent, or else he would be afraid that I might smell it. Now what fruit without much scent is in season just now?

"When I know that I shall have guessed the riddle!"

Moti was a country lad, and used to work in his father's garden. He knew all the common fruits, so he thought he ought to be able to guess right; but not to let it seem too easy, he gazed up at the ceiling with a puzzled expression, looked at the floor with an air of wisdom, his fingers pressed against his forehead, and then he said, slowly, with his eyes on the king:

"It is freshly plucked! It is round and it is red! It is a pomegranate!"

Now the King knew nothing about fruits except that they were good to eat; and, as for seasons, he asked for whatever fruit he wanted whenever he wanted it, and saw that he got it; so to him Moti's guess was like a miracle, and clear proof not only of his wisdom but of his innocence, for it *was* a pomegranate that he had put into the box!

Of course when the King marveled and praised Moti's wisdom, everybody else did so, too; and, whilst the horsetraders went off crestfallen, Moti took the horse and entered the King's service.

Very soon after this, Moti, who continued to live in the serai, came back one wet and stormy evening to find that his precious horse had strayed. Nothing remained of him but a broken halter cord, and no one knew what had become of him. After inquiring

"It Is a Pomegranate!"

of everyone who was likely to know, Moti seized the cord and his big staff and sallied out to look for him.

Away and away he tramped out of the city and into the neighboring forest, tracking hoof-marks in the mud.

Presently it grew late, but still Moti wandered on until suddenly in the gathering darkness he came right upon a tiger who was contentedly eating his horse.

"You thief!" shrieked Moti, and ran up, and, just as the tiger, in astonishment, dropped a bone — *whack* came Moti's staff on his head with such good will that the beast was half-stunned and could hardly breathe or see. Then Moti continued to shower upon him blows and abuse until the poor tiger could hardly stand, whereupon Moti tied the broken halter round his neck and dragged him back to the serai.

"If you had my horse," he said, "I will at least have you, that's fair enough!" And he tied him up securely by the head and heels, much as he used to tie the horse; then, the night being far gone, he flung himself beside him and slept soundly.

You cannot imagine anything like the fright of the people in the serai, when they woke up and found a tiger — very battered but still a tiger — securely tethered amongst themselves and their beasts!

Men gathered in groups talking and exclaiming, and finding fault with the innkeeper for allowing such a dangerous beast into the serai, and all the while the innkeeper was just as troubled as the

"You Thief!"

rest, and none dared go near the place where the tiger stood blinking miserably on everyone, and where Moti lay stretched out snoring like thunder.

At last news reached the King that Moti had exchanged his horse for a live tiger; and the monarch himself came down, half disbelieving the tale, to see if it were really true. Someone at last awaked Moti with the news that his royal master was come; and he arose yawning, and was soon delightedly explaining and showing off his new possession.

The King, however, did not share his pleasure at all, but called up a soldier to shoot the tiger, much to the relief of all the inmates of the serai except Moti.

If the King, however, was before convinced that Moti was one of the wisest of men, he was now still more convinced that he was the bravest, and he increased his pay a hundredfold, so that our hero thought that he was the *luckiest* of men.

A week or two after this incident the King sent for Moti, who on arrival found his master in despair. A neighboring monarch, he explained, who had many more soldiers than he, had declared war against him, and he was at his wits' end, for he had neither money enough to buy him off nor soldiers enough to fight him — what was he to do?

"If that is all, don't you trouble," said Moti. "Turn out your men, and I'll go with them, and we'll soon bring this robber to reason."

The Monarch Himself Came Down.

How Moti Won The War

The King began to revive at these hopeful words, and took Moti off to his stable where he bade him choose for himself any horse he liked. There were plenty of fine horses in the stalls, but to the King's astonishment Moti chose a poor little rat of a pony that was used to carry grass and water for the rest of the stable.

"But why do you choose that beast?" said the King.

"Well, you see, your majesty," replied Moti, "there are so many chances that I may fall off, and if I choose one of your fine big horses I shall have so far to fall that I shall probably break my leg or my arm, if not my neck, but if I fall off this little beast I can't hurt myself much."

A very comical sight was Moti when he rode out to the war. The only weapon he carried was his staff, and to help him to keep his balance on horseback he had tied to each of his ankles a big stone that nearly touched the ground as he sat astride the little pony.

The rest of the King's cavalry were not very numerous, but they pranced along in armor on fine horses. Behind them came a great rabble of men on foot armed with all sorts of weapons, and last of all was the King with his attendants, very nervous and ill at ease. So the army started.

They had not very far to go, but Moti's little pony, weighted with a heavy man and two big rocks, soon began to lag behind the cavalry, and would have lagged behind the infantry too, only they were not very anxious to be too early in the fight, and hung back so as to give Moti plenty of time.

A Poor Little Rat of a Pony

How Moti Won The War

Moti jogged along more and more slowly for some time, until at last, getting impatient at the slowness of the pony, he gave him such a tremendous thwack with his staff that the pony completely lost his temper and bolted. First one stone became untied and rolled away in a cloud of dust to one side of the road, whilst Moti nearly rolled off, too, but he clasped his steed valiantly by its ragged mane, and, dropping his staff, held on for dear life.

Then fortunately the other rock broke away from his other leg and rolled thunderously down a neighboring ravine. Meanwhile the advanced cavalry had barely time to draw to one side when Moti came dashing by, yelling bloodthirsty threats to his pony: "You wait till I get hold of you! I'll skin you alive! I'll wring your neck! I'll break every bone in your body!"

The cavalry thought that this dreadful language was meant for the enemy, and were filled with admiration for his courage. Many of their horses were quite upset by this whirlwind that galloped howling through their midst, and in a few minutes, after a little plunging and rearing and kicking, the whole troop were following on Moti's heels.

Far in advance, Moti continued his wild career. Presently he came to a great field of castor-oil plants, ten or twelve feet high, big and bushy, but quite green and soft. Hoping to escape from the back of his fiery steed, Moti grasped one in passing, but its roots gave way, and he dashed on, with the whole plant looking like a young tree flourishing in his grip!

The Pony Bolted.

How Moti Won The War

The enemy was in battle array, advancing over the plain, their King with them confident and cheerful, when suddenly from the front came a desperate rider at a furious gallop.

"Sire!" he cried, "Save yourself! The enemy is coming!"

"What *do* you mean?" said the King.

"Oh, sire!" panted the messenger, "Fly at once, there is no time to lose. Foremost of the enemy rides a mad giant at a furious gallop. He flourishes a tree for a club and is wild with anger, for as he goes he cries: 'You wait till I get hold of you! I'll skin you alive! I'll wring your neck! I'll break every bone in your body!' Others ride behind, and you will do well to retire before this whirlwind of destruction comes upon you!"

Just then out of a cloud of dust in the distance, the King saw Moti approaching at a hard gallop, looking indeed like a giant compared with the little beast he rode, whirling his castor-oil plant, which in the distance might have seemed an oak tree, and the sound of his revilings and shoutings came down upon the breeze!

Behind him the dust cloud moved to the sound of the thunder of hoofs, whilst here and there flashed the glitter of steel. The sight and the sound struck terror into the King, and, turning his horse, he fled at top speed, thinking that a regiment of yelling giants was upon him; and all his force followed him as fast as they might go.

One fat officer alone could not keep up on foot with that mad rush, and as Moti came galloping up he flung himself on the

"Sire! Save Yourself!"

ground in abject fear. This was too much for Moti's excited pony, who shied so suddenly that Moti went flying over his head like a sky rocket, and alighted right on the top of his fat foe.

Quickly regaining his feet, Moti began to swing his plant round his head and to shout:

"Where are your men? Bring them up and I'll kill them. My regiments! Come on, the whole lot of you! Where's your King? Bring him to me. Here are all my fine fellows coming up and we'll each pull up a tree by the roots and lay you all flat and your houses and towns and everything else! Come on!"

But the poor fat officer could do nothing but squat on his knees with his hands together, gasping. At last, when he got his breath, Moti sent him off to bring his King, and to tell him that if he was reasonable his life should be spared.

Off the poor man went, and by the time the troops of Moti's side had come up and arranged themselves to look as formidable as possible, he returned with his King. The latter was very humble and apologetic, and promised never to make war any more, to pay a large sum of money, and altogether do whatever his conqueror wished.

So the armies on both sides went rejoicing home, and this was really the making of the fortune of clumsy Moti, who lived long and contrived always to be looked up to as a fountain of wisdom, valor, and discretion by all except his own relatives, who could never understand what he had done to be considered so much wiser than anyone else!

Moti the Wise